Eyes Only for You

"Andrew Grey is truly a spectacular author and writes books that make an impact on the readers."

—Gay Book Reviews

"It was hot and frustrating and sweet. Also quite romantic. Many things that make an Andrew Grey book great!"

—Diverse Reader

Can't Live Without You

"This story was so fresh and new—and so well written and planned out, it was a pleasure to read from beginning to end."

—Alpha Book Club

"Sweet, wonderful characters who overcome their sad past and find a way to carve a future together."

—Hearts on Fire Reviews

Turning the Page

"The story telling is straightforward, the character of Malcolm relatable, and the ending—with a surprise twist and an element of danger—is quite satisfying."

—Gay.Guy.Reading and Friends

"The story was told very realistically. I felt for these characters."

—Two Chicks Obsessed

More praise for
ANDREW GREY

The Lone Rancher

"This story has an intriguing plot with twists and turns in just about every chapter and was real enough to make it believable… A hot sexy read by the fabulous Andrew Grey."

—Bike Book Reviews

Chasing the Dream

"This is a wonderful story of a reverse rags-to-riches."

—The Blogger Girls

"I loved it from beginning to end!"

—Rainbow Book Reviews

Rekindled Flame

"Definitely a well done and uplifting story."

—My Fiction Nook

"*Rekindled Flame* is another well written story from Andrew Grey. There's danger and suspense and, as always, there's that great feeling of camaraderie, support and a sweet HEA."

—The Novel Approach

By ANDREW GREY

Published by DREAMSPINNER PRESS
www.dreamspinnerpress.com

By ANDREW GREY (CONT.)

Published by DREAMSPINNER PRESS
www.dreamspinnerpress.com

NOBLE INTENTIONS

ANDREW GREY

DREAMSPINNER PRESS

Published by

DREAMSPINNER PRESS

5032 Capital Circle SW, Suite 2, PMB# 279, Tallahassee, FL 32305-7886 USA
www.dreamspinnerpress.com

Noble Intentions
© 2016 Andrew Grey.

Cover Art
© 2016 L.C. Chase.
http://www.lcchase.com
Cover content is for illustrative purposes only and any person depicted on the cover is a model.

ISBN: 978-1-63533-122-6
Digital ISBN: 978-1-63533-123-3
Library of Congress Control Number: 2016913755
Published December 2016
v. 1.1

Printed in the United States of America
∞
This paper meets the requirements of
ANSI/NISO Z39.48-1992 (Permanence of Paper).

To Elizabeth. Remember, dear, you were the one who asked for it.

CHAPTER 1

"ROBERT," HIS aide, Blake, said as he knocked on the frame beside the open door to Robert's tiny office.

"Am I late for another meeting?" Robert looked up from his computer, where he'd been preparing the documents on a case for a client whose landlord was trying to evict her improperly. The guy was a real piece of work, and Robert was determined to win her some relief from the local council.

Blake chuckled softly. "No."

Robert breathed a sigh of relief and continued typing as fast as he could. He was scheduled to meet with the council in less than an hour, and he wanted to make sure he had all his arguments in place.

"But there is someone here to see you. A solicitor from London." Blake sounded half-breathless with excitement—probably wondering what was going on and if he could increase his stature in the office rumor mill.

Robert closed his eyes and tried to think if he had had any business or clients that would precipitate a visit from a colleague in London. Robert was technically a barrister, trained to argue cases in front of the courts. But here on the edge of Cornwall, Robert had decided that rather than go into high-powered practice in London, he'd become an advocate for those without the means to advocate for themselves. So he'd gone into practice with a few like-minded friends from school, and they'd opened their office on the second floor of a run-down building in Smithford. In their practice, they took everything and did everything. Two of his partners were solicitors, and Robert had learned the ins and outs of that profession as well.

"Give me five minutes, please."

1

Blake nodded, and Robert put the last touches on the argument and then saved the file. He'd just finished when Blake led in a man about Robert's age, spit-and-polished, wearing a suit that cost as much as Robert made in a month. Robert stood to meet the man.

"Robert Morton? William Montgomery. I'm here on behalf of your uncle, the Earl of Hantford."

"My uncle…." Robert didn't honestly remember having an uncle, but then again, his mother's family had not been the most accommodating when she'd married Robert's father. No one had talked about his mother's family in so long that they didn't register immediately in his memory. "Yes…?"

"Yes. Your uncle, Lord Harrison Hantford, the Earl of Hantford…." He paused. "Apparently the family changed their last name to that of the estate some six generations ago. He recently passed away, and under his will, you are his heir. The estate is entailed, which means your uncle didn't have a great deal of choice in the matter. You are his closest living male heir, and as such you are entitled to the earldom, as well as all the property associated with it."

Robert shivered slightly and blinked in near disbelief. He motioned for Mr. Montgomery to sit down, remembering his manners through the complete shock. "So you're saying I'm the Earl of Hantford now?" He sank into his chair and wondered what kind of holy hell had befallen him.

"Yes, sir. Or I should say, your lordship." Mr. Montgomery seemed to be taking little delight in this.

"Did you know my uncle?" Robert asked.

"I'm afraid I didn't. He was a client with Rhodes, Wentworth, and Middleton for many years, and the task of notifying you fell to me."

"I see." Robert's analytical mind began to kick in. "So what exactly has my uncle left me?"

"There is the family estate, Ashton Park, and a home in London. I'm at a loss to tell you much about them. I haven't seen either property myself, but I will be happy to meet you in the coming weeks to take you to visit them, as well as discuss any arrangements you'd like to make for the properties and contents," Mr. Montgomery said, very businesslike, which was both a relief and unsettling for Robert.

"Can you tell me if the estate is healthy?"

Mr. Montgomery chose that moment to break eye contact, and immediately Robert knew the answer. "I don't know the particulars, but I am under the impression that your uncle lived in the home in London and that he rarely visited Ashton Park. As to more details on the state of the place, we'll have to assess that when we go see it." It was a diplomatic answer, which probably meant that he'd just inherited a huge money-sucking country house with very little means to support it.

"All right." Robert had no idea in hell what else to say. He was a man who made his living with words, and he was at a near complete loss. "Thank you so very much."

"Would you like to meet tomorrow? I can at least take you to Ashton Park so you can see it. I will also have a number of papers and documents that I will need you to sign."

"Is there anyone else who has a potential claim on the estate?" Robert asked.

"No. Your uncle married, but the earl and his wife had no children. I understand from the more senior colleagues in my firm that that was a great sorrow to both of them. However, other than a few impressions and details, I don't have much information to give you. The earl's business was handled by one of our partners who recently passed away unexpectedly, and I'm stepping in to try to fill his rather large shoes." Mr. Montgomery sounded excited about this opportunity, but Robert also saw a touch of fear in his eyes, which would help keep him on his toes. Robert understood that kind of fear; he experienced it on a regular basis. Failure could be lurking everywhere, so it was to be guarded against and held at bay by always being at one's very best.

"All right." Robert pulled up his calendar and figured he could clear part of his schedule for the following day. He arranged a time, and Mr. Montgomery left his office.

Somehow Robert managed to get his mind back on his work, but not without a great deal of effort.

THAT EVENING, after a successful local council meeting that granted him everything he had wanted for his client, Robert pulled up to his mother's small cottage on the outskirts of town. She and his father had saved for years to buy their dream home. His mother, who was approaching seventy, still tended the garden and lovingly cared for the house the way she always had and showed no signs of slowing down.

"How was your day?" She gave him a fright when she popped up from behind one of the garden gateposts, where she had apparently been wrestling with some stubborn weeds.

"God." He stepped back and took a breath to still his heart. "It's getting a little late to be working out here, Mum."

"Pish," she said dismissively. "When you're as old as I am, you take your bursts of energy when you can get them." She dropped the weeds she was holding on the pile she'd collected. "Let's have a cup of tea."

"Good idea." He followed her inside and sat on one of the kitchen chairs, watching his mother put a kettle on. He remembered the dining room furniture from when he was a child. His father had made the table and chairs for his mother as a wedding present, and they had been a part of the family for as long as he could remember.

"What brings you by?" She plugged in the electric kettle and got down the cups and pot so they would be ready.

"It seems that your brother passed away."

She patted the table a few times. "Harrison is dead." She said the words in the same tone that she did when she talked about her neighbor, who she referred to as "the damned old randy bastard"

4

on a regular basis. She smiled for a second and then turned to him. "Christ on the cross."

"You got it in one, Mum."

"But I was disinherited, and…." She sank into the chair across from him. "So my arse of a brother ended up with what he wanted anyway."

"Excuse me?" Robert said, trying to follow all of this.

"My brother was many things—pompous, arrogant, a pain in the arse know-it-all who thought since he had the title, he also had the right to make decisions for everyone else." The kettle was done, and she got up and poured. Robert waited until she was ready to continue. She brought the tea tray with pot and cups to the table and set it down gently. She filled the cups, knowing already how he took it, and handed him his. "My parents died when I was nineteen. So Harrison inherited the title and became head of the family. He thought two things. First, that the title gave him the right to dictate everything about my life. And second, that we'd stepped back a hundred years and that he ruled the damn roost, as well as my personal life. The idiot." She took a sip, pinkie out, as genteel as possible.

"Why didn't I ever hear any of this before?"

She set down her cup. "I dated a friend of my brother's for five years. He was also titled, with a lot of money. Harrison was so excited. He thought we'd marry, but the reason we dated for so long was because I wasn't ready. Then I met your father. George, the guy my brother wanted me to marry, was as pompous as Harrison. He'd hired your father to do some restoration work at his home, and I took one look at him and that was it. Your father stole my heart with a wink, a smile, and one peek at his gorgeous backside." She giggled, and Robert was glad he didn't have a mouthful of tea at that moment.

"So you dumped George and married Dad."

"Yes. In a way. I announced that I wasn't going to marry George and that I loved Peter with all my heart, and Harrison went into a rage. He was always a control freak. Now I think he was deranged and needed professional help. But he hadn't gotten any then. When I didn't back down, he disowned me, and I turned my back on the arsehole forever."

"Mum, I think you're losing me a little."

"I'm getting to the good part. See, Harrison married soon after that, and they supposedly settled down into wedded bliss. But it seemed Harrison had bigger problems. His plumbing wasn't completely functional, and he could never have children." She snickered. "Served the old jackass right, and it's a blessing for the human race. At least his bastardness won't be passed on to anyone else." There was no mistaking her sense of glee at the turn of events.

"Mum!" He had never heard such vehemence from his mother.

"He had the audacity to approach me about returning to the family after your father died—if I let him groom you to take over for him. I told him to stuff it. You had your own life and didn't need the mess that he wanted to heap on you." She sighed. "But he did it anyway. If he weren't dead, I'd wring his neck."

"When was that?"

"About five years ago. He was in one of those regretful phases, but I knew it was a load of garden fertilizer. He never did anything without getting something for himself. And your father had just died, and I thought he was trying to take you from me and…." Her lower lip quivered, and Robert stood to gently place his hands on her shoulders. His mother was many things, but touchy-feely wasn't one of them. She placed a hand on his, and Robert gave her a chance to compose herself.

"Why didn't you tell me any of this before?"

"Because I didn't want you to have anything to do with him. Harrison was an awful man, and we had a good life here. Your father was an amazing provider. He worked hard and made his furniture to help ensure we had some of the extras." She squeezed his hand once, then dropped hers and looked up at him. "I wasn't—"

"It's okay, Mum." Robert waited for her to take a breath. "I wish you had told me, but you're right. We had a good life, and if your brother was as big a jackass as you describe, then we were better off without him."

"But now you're the Earl of Hantford."

"It seems so."

"And everything that goes with it." She turned back to her tea. "I tried to keep you from all that. I really did."

He wasn't sure what his mother was referring to, but it only added to his sense of nervousness. "I'm meeting the solicitor tomorrow, and we're going to the estate. Do you want to come with me?" *It would be really nice not to go alone.* "I'll understand if you'd rather not."

"Where are you meeting him?"

"At my office at one."

"Then I'll go with you. We can meet for lunch, and I'll tell you what I know about what you'll be walking into. Granted, my information is a little out-of-date." She motioned for him to sit, and Robert complied and finished his tea. "This is a burden I had hoped to try to spare you."

"Mum, I'm an earl and I have a peerage.... It's—"

"A burden unlike anything I think you understand." She sighed. "All I wanted for you was a life filled with happiness and the ability to make your own decisions and live your life the way you wanted. Harrison never understood that. He always thought his way of thinking was the only way and that everyone wanted the same things he did. Now he's pulled you into the mess I'm sure he created."

"We don't know the state of things."

"No, we don't. But we're going to find out." She poured another cup of tea, stood, and opened a nearby cupboard. She pulled out a bottle of whiskey and dumped a healthy dollop into her tea.

Things must have been bad. There had been only one other time that he'd seen his mother do that, and it had been the morning of

7

his father's funeral. She had said that she needed some false courage to get through that day, and it seemed she required another dose.

"I'll see you for lunch, though I suspect I'm not going to have much of an appetite."

"I doubt things are as bad as all that." Robert stood and kissed her on the cheek before leaving the cottage. He stopped in the garden on the way out, admiring some of her flowers in the late evening light, and then walked to his car.

ROBERT FELT as though he had been through a meat grinder. He hadn't slept all night and had gone into the office early so he could get as much done as possible. He'd worked with Blake to rearrange his schedule so he could have the afternoon out of the office. Of course, with his mother in the car, he wasn't able to make calls the way he normally would.

The estate was nearly an hour west from Smithford, and he followed William's black hearselike car. His mother had been surprisingly quiet for much of the trip until they turned a corner and the top of a turret broke the skyline.

"That's it."

"When was the last time you were here?"

"Just before I married your father, so over forty years ago." She gasped when Robert made the turn and the estate came into view.

William pulled to the side of the road, and Robert followed. He parked, got out of the car, and walked up to William. His mother decided she wanted to stay where she was.

"That's Ashton Park." William waved his hands in all directions.

"How much land is there with the place?" Robert asked.

"A lot. It's the one true asset of the earldom. There is plenty of land, and from what I can gather from my colleague's notes, your uncle refused to sell any of it, no matter how difficult things got."

"How badly is the place mortgaged?" Robert asked, afraid as hell of the answer. He expected it to be up to the rafters.

"That's the thing. We can't find any record of one anywhere."

"What? You mean I own this pile free and clear?" How in the hell could that be possible? There had to be a catch, and in the back of his mind, Robert latched on to exactly what it could be. "The taxes. Forget I asked."

"Yes, sir. They are going to be steep on the manor house and all the land. However, since your uncle managed to pay the inheritance duties from when he received the estate, you only have the ones to pay for this transfer of ownership."

Like that was a comfort. Instantly upon his uncle's death, Robert owed millions in death taxes on a place he hadn't known existed, other than in some picture he might have seen on one of those documentaries they did on country houses and such.

"Well, we may as well see just how bad a state the old place is in." He tried to think of what he was going to do with it. Selling was the first thing that came to mind—if that were even possible.

"Yes, my lord," William said, and Robert stopped him.

"I'm Robert. Please call me that. I'm not going to stand on all the ceremony and crap, okay? I was Robert before you told me this news and I'm still Robert now."

"Okay." William smiled for the first time. "I'll do whatever I can, Robert."

Robert turned back to the estate and groaned. "Let's go see what we're dealing with." He got back in the car and followed William through the old gate and up the weed-scattered drive, toward the front door. "This place is...." Robert didn't quite know what to say.

"I grew up here," his mother said. "This was my home for much of my younger years."

Robert stopped, and they both got out, the gravel crunching under their feet. The façade of the building looked to be in fine shape. The stone was discolored but appeared intact.

"Is there anyone here?" Robert asked.

"Yes. There is a caretaker on the property. He lives in one of the other homes on the property and sees to it that the building itself remains in reasonable care. But little else seems to have been done in some time." William produced a huge set of keys that looked like something to open a medieval jail. He unlocked the front door and held it open for Robert and his mother.

Robert stepped inside and gasped. All the shutters had been drawn, and everything was covered in sheets and drapes that looked like dusty old ghosts as the breeze from outside fluttered into the hall. Paintings, chandeliers—everything was draped and covered. But even under the dust and sheets, the grandeur of the entry hall shone through.

"My God."

"This used to be…." His mother came inside. "I remember greeting guests as they arrived. Your grandparents were very social people and loved to entertain. It's what this house was built for. Harrison used to love his parties as well, but his took on a very different tone." She walked to the left and pushed open the door to a paneled living room with heavy molding, where a rug lay rolled up to one side. More sheet ghosts and drapes covered everything, and the floor was so dusty, it was hard to see the wood.

Robert looked up and gasped at the frescoed ceiling. "At least that's in one piece. How could anyone just leave all this to rot?" He moved into the living room and through to the next, which was a bookless library.

"What happened to everything? These shelves were full." His mother sounded as though she were going to cry as she wiped her fingers through decades of dust on an empty shelf.

"Apparently they were moved to some sort of storage," William said. "There was a bill for it in the estate records."

Robert lifted his gaze once again and knew the reason for moving stuff to storage. The expansive coffered ceiling was pockmarked with yellow stains. He closed his eyes and groaned. "The roof is going. Some of those stains are recent."

"I did me best, my lord."

Robert turned to find a man in his fifties standing in the doorway, hat bunched in his hands. "Robert Morton." He held out his hand, and the man who Robert assumed was the caretaker stepped forward nervously.

"Gene Parget, my lord. I noticed the room was leaking, so I went up and patched it best I could. I think I stopped the water coming in for now. But some damage was done, mainly in the bedroom above this one. But I don't think I can patch it much more. It needs replacing."

"What about the electrics?" Robert asked.

"That and the plumbing are going too, sir. I don't like to turn on the lights because...." He shrugged. "And the water is off to the entire manor in case of leaks."

"So what you're telling me is that this huge pile of a place needs electrics, plumbing, a roof, as well as...." He raised his eyebrows. "Is there anything that's in good shape?"

"The walls, sir. They're thick and strong, and I repaired the windows last year. Took out the bad ones, reglazed them, and then put them back. I do that every other year."

"What about the kitchen and bathrooms?" When Gene just looked down at the floor, Robert had his answer, and God knew what in the hell he was going to do. "Please show us the rest of the house, and don't leave anything out," he told Gene.

His mother moved back into the living room as Gene led Robert out of the library.

Gene showed him room after room of haunting neglect. Wallpaper peeled from many of the upstairs bedrooms, and the nursery sat frozen in time, like it was waiting for children that had gone and were never coming back. "The summer is humid and the winter cold. I did me best to care for the place, but I'm just me and—"

"It's all right, Gene. You have done the best you could, I'm sure. No one is blaming you for this." He sighed as he looked at the dust and grime covering dinge and neglect.

"Yes, my lord."

"Don't call me that, please." He was never going to get used to that. "I'm Robert. I may have inherited a title, but I believe that men should earn respect, not be given it because they happen to have been born into the right family." Robert turned and wandered through the last rooms, seeing more of the same. The room above the library was the worst so far. The plaster was cracked severely, and parts of the ceiling were in need of stabilization. He didn't go inside and closed the door after a quick peek. "Let's go back down. I think I've seen enough. What other buildings are there on the grounds?"

"There are the stables, which are empty. There's the motorshed, which is also empty. There were greenhouses, but they have fallen down. There are cottages in the village that are part of the estate. They have tenants, and part of their rent agreement requires that they maintain them. I've ensured that has happened. Then there is the park, the thousands of acres around the manor."

Robert nodded, trying to make sense of all this. Mostly what he'd inherited was a money pit. Yes, it wasn't mortgaged, and maybe he could do that, but then he needed the place to generate revenue, which wasn't going to happen with it in this condition.

"Thank you," he said absently. He'd seen more than enough of the mess his uncle had heaped on him.

He met his mother in the hallway, where she peered under sheets and dustcovers. He caught her eye and nodded, and they made their way to the door.

"I know this is a lot to take in and it's going to take some time to get the estate settled," William said as they walked out the front door.

"I know. Not that it's going to make a great deal of difference." Robert needed to figure out what in the hell he was going to do with a place that was so out of step with any sort of modern lifestyle that it threatened to raise a headache the size of London. "Gene, thank you for everything you've done and continue to do. I appreciate it." He shook the caretaker's hand once again and then led his mother to his car. He got in and lowered his window as William approached.

"I'd like to review the rest of the estate details with you soon. There is the house in London, as well as a few other assets."

"Please tell me there is some money somewhere to do something with all this." As overwhelming as all this was, he wasn't above begging if necessary.

"There is enough in various trusts to continue what your uncle was doing. The principal in the trusts can't be touched and it provides an income. I believe that pays for the caretaker and the storage of the books and things. But other than that, no. What money your uncle had, he left to someone else." At that moment, William was as stoic as any good lawyer had to be.

"Okay. I'll need to catch up. Can we meet on Monday?"

William nodded, stepped back from the car, and went to lock the front door of the house.

Robert slowly pulled away. As he drove through the gate, the weight on his chest lifted slightly, but not very much. "What do I do with it?" Robert asked.

"The rooms are still furnished. Almost all of it is still there," she said with a sense of awe.

"All of what?"

"That manor has been in our family for ten generations. You are the eleventh, and the things they collected over the years were all added to the manor. I was afraid Harrison would have sold them, but that probably took more energy than he was willing to spend. So it's all there."

"Okay." Robert turned onto the road back to his office. "So I could sell the furnishings, and break up the land and sell that as well. That would pay the taxes and leave an empty building that could be sold or added to the National Trust if I could get them to take it." He glanced at his mother, who looked about to cry.

"That's your history, my history, and you'd do that without a second thought?" She wiped her eyes, and Robert tried to remember the last time he'd seen his mother cry. He had a hard time doing it. She never cried—stiff upper lip and all that. "You can't just throw it away offhand."

"Then what do I do? I can mortgage the place to the hilt and try to do the repairs that need to be made, but how in the hell do I pay the money back? The estate doesn't have much income, and I can't just open it to tourists and have them flock to the place like it was Downton Abbey. A few people might come, but not enough to make it worthwhile. I could just donate the whole thing to the National Trust and make it their headache, but then everything would be gone." And that was going to break his mother's heart. He could see that.

Robert pulled to a stop at an intersection and waited for a truck loaded with hay to pass before making the turn and continuing on.

"There has to be a way to do something." She was thinking already, he could tell.

"I'm going to have to see what else I've inherited and then try to figure out what can be done." Thankfully the estate wasn't too far away from where he and his mother lived. He could at least continue to live without having to make commutes halfway across the country. "I'm not going to make any decisions today or tomorrow." Robert grew quiet as he drove the rest of the way back to his office.

"I've been thinking," his mother said with a weird smile that Robert was having trouble reading. "You need money to fix up the estate, and you also have a title."

"Okay. I have a title that doesn't help me, other than make me sound like a toff."

His mother leaned closer. "That title comes with a peerage and it has power. People respect the titles. Good or bad, they do, and the title has value."

"Okay. So do I sell it?" Robert asked, knowing he was being ridiculous.

"Of course not. Well, maybe in a way. You do what the aristocracy has always done when they needed money. You marry it."

Robert turned off the engine and blinked in disbelief. "You know I'm gay, Mum. I'm not going to marry a woman."

"No. But I bet there is a gay man with a lot of money who would marry you for the chance to become a count." She held up her hand. "Wives of earls are countesses, so the husband of an earl could be a count. Think about it. All you have to do is find someone who wants a title and marry him. Of course, he'd have to have piles of money, but you're an earl. Meeting people with money shouldn't be a problem."

He knew his mother was falling in love with the idea. The only problem was that she wasn't the one who was going to have to marry someone for money. Granted, he hadn't had much luck in the love-life department, but still he wasn't particularly interested in selling himself so he could fix up some family estate he hadn't known existed until a few days ago.

"Mum. That's crazy."

"No, it's not. I'm not saying you need to marry some prig you hate. But think about it. Earls and dukes have been doing this sort of thing for centuries. Who knows what you could get out of it? We got bloody Churchill from that kind of relationship. His mother was an American heiress." The more she warmed up to the idea, the more Robert wanted to crawl under the car and hide.

"That's enough. Like I said, I need to see what's in the estate and what my options are before I throw myself off the arranged marriage cliff."

"Who says it's an arranged marriage? There are dating sites and things like that on the Internet. We'll simply find you a gay matchmaker or something, like that show on American television." Her excitement made him more uncomfortable by the second. Where had this idea come from and how did he get it out of her head? "You go ahead and look into the estate. I'm going to go look into some things on my end."

"Mum. Just stop this whole thing right now. I'll come up with a plan to try to figure out what I'm going to do after my trip to the

States. I don't need your help getting myself married off to some rich guy for his money. That isn't the kind of life that I want. None of this is."

He could see how his entire way of life was about to change. Up until then it had been the law firm and trying to help people who couldn't help themselves. And now he was supposed to be the Earl of Hantford and all that entailed, including looking after a huge pile of a house because it had been in his family… the family that had disowned his mother. This whole thing rubbed him the wrong way, and all he wanted was a way out of this mess. Selling everything seemed like that way to go. He could be rid of it and that would be that. Pay the taxes, put the rest in trust for the next generation, wherever that would come from, and say to hell with it all.

One look at his mother's set jaw and the gleam in her eyes told him that wasn't going to happen. Not even close. Lord help him—he was going to need it.

CHAPTER 2

"DANIEL," JOANNE said from next to his desk.

He looked up from the computer screen where he was studying order throughput and fulfillment from his desk at his New York office.

His tap at the screen stopped whatever she was going to say. "Look at this. There is something about this item that is getting hung up in the system every time someone orders it." He continued watching.

"The two-tone low-rise boot," she said with authority. "Systems is already looking into it. They said it's a record issue and they'll have it fixed in—"

Ding.

Daniel smiled as the problem was resolved and the backlog of orders cleared. "Thanks."

"They said they're looking into how the issue got into the system, and they'll close the hole today." She smiled.

Joanne was the savior of his sanity. And that was why he'd made her his assistant and Woman Friday. He'd said Girl Friday once, referring to the movie, and the look she'd thrown his way threatened to end global warming and bring on the next ice age.

"Awesome." He shifted his gaze from his screen to her. "What can I do for you? Am I supposed to be somewhere I'm not?" He was usually on top of his schedule, but Joanne always had it under control, especially when he got deep into one of his idea phases.

"You have fifteen minutes, and then you need to meet with the visual imaging department. They have designs for the splash pages that you need to review and approve before noon today. You also have a call from Philip at Heartland waiting for you."

Daniel grabbed the edge of his desk in a death grip. He prided himself on always being as cool and collected at work as possible. He firmly believed that if he showed the stress and pressure he was under, the rest of the team would feel it as well, and he wanted them at their best… and that meant free to think and innovate. Still, those people at Heartland Shoes could try the patience of Mother Teresa.

"Don't they ever stop?" He picked up the phone. "Daniel Fabian," he said in his most pleasant tone.

"It's Phillip Wilson over at Heartland. How's it going?" He always started every conversation as though they were the best of friends.

"I'm great here. How are you?" Daniel asked as though he didn't already know what they wanted.

"Great!" Phillip said with enough false enthusiasm to make a cheerleader retch. "Did you have a chance to look over our latest offer?"

Daniel glanced toward the trash where he'd dropped his copy. "Yes, I did."

"And…?"

"No, thank you." He was as polite as his mama—may she rest in peace because she never got any in life—had always told him to be. "I've said it more than once: I'm not interested in selling to you or anyone. I thank you for your interest." God, the sugar that dripped from his mouth. He hated these people and knew that once they got their hands on what he'd built, they'd take it apart piece by piece.

Silence on the other end. "We'd really like to take your company to the next level."

"We'll get there on our own and in a way that's healthy." Daniel had done amazing things. Growing up in Texas, he'd always been about the boots. So when he got the idea to expand the line of footwear into colors, styles, and textures that no one else had dreamed of, he'd hit on a gold mine. Kick in the Pants was a runaway success, and they had just added the icing on the cake. They'd developed a way to have customers scan their feet so they could order custom boots made especially for them. The innovation was already a sensation.

"Daniel…." The tone went deeper. "We'd love to add your technology to our line of brick-and-mortar stores. We already have people researching a way to do it."

Daniel had been expecting something like this. It was how Heartland Shoes operated. "Everything about our process is patented and copyrighted so tight, an ant can't get past us. I have lawyers who are watching for any copycats and are ready to shut them down in an instant. You can go ahead and try, but if it even looks close to us, we'll have you slapped with an injunction so fast, you'll wonder why your butt hurts."

"We have people too, and—"

"I know who your people are and who you think you're going to hire. I did my homework, and you'll find they're already on retainer. So threatening me is going to get you run over as flat as an armadillo in the wake of a semi. You may think I'm some geek you can push around, but I'm from Texas, and I make and sell boots, so I know how to kick ass."

He did other things as well. Kick in the Pants was only the latest in his string of Internet successes, but it was the one these assholes wanted, and he wasn't going to give it up. He had a store that sold all kinds of western fashions—definitely not your daddy's western apparel. They were taking on the international fashion establishment and making them take notice. He also had developed a women's fashion line with his sister that was making a name among the major department stores. Daniel was no lightweight, and he wasn't going to be pushed around. There had been plenty of that in his past, and it wasn't going to be part of his present or future if he could help it.

"I think it's time for you to go back and lick your wounds. Find someone else to buy because we aren't interested. And making threats isn't the way to go."

"We don't lose…," Phillip said gruffly.

"You will this time. Now, I have one more thing to say. If you want to press this, there are social media outlets that we will take to with a vengeance, and people love us." Daniel smiled. They had built up a following that was second to none. "So don't threaten me or my businesses." He grinned to himself. "And for the record, I seriously considered your offer, but you just validated that I made the right decision. So you have a nice day." He hung up and sat back in his chair.

Joanne returned like an assistant-in-the-box. "Is Heartland dead?"

"As a doornail."

"You have another call, but I'm not sure what to do with it. It's a Steven Rhys-Jones. I swear that's how he introduced himself." She held up her hands in a "swear to God" gesture. "He said you knew him from Lipton."

A cold sweat broke out, and Daniel had no idea why. "Thanks. Put it through." He wasn't sure why he was getting this call unless it was some kind of drive for a donation. "Hello?"

"Danny Boy," Steven said in a singsongy voice that took Daniel back to prep school in the worst way possible. Those two words had come to mean either teasing, hazing, or teenage torture. Daniel had never known which, and he'd hated it.

His visceral reaction brought a cringe to his lips. "Stevey," he said in return, pushing away the bile that threatened to rise. "What's up?"

"We've been putting together this whole reunion thing, and no one could find you."

Somehow Daniel didn't believe that, but he let it go.

"It's in two months, July 15th, at the Plaza in New York. An invitation was sent to the last address we had, but it came back. So I said I'd try to look up and call my old pal Danny Boy."

"That was nice of you, Stevey. What have you been up to?"

"Oh, went on to law school and joined the family firm. The old man retired, so now I'm running the whole thing. One of the biggest in Albany." He sounded so proud and far from the bully who had tormented the hell out of Daniel. Why Stevey had to be the one to call was beyond Daniel. There weren't many people from that time in his life that he wanted to talk to at all, and Stevey had to be one of the last people on earth.

"That's good. Why don't you forward me the invitation?" He rattled off a Gmail address he rarely looked at, figuring that was safe and he wouldn't get a shitload of spam and money requests crossing his desk on a regular basis. "I'd appreciate it."

"No problem, Danny Boy. I'll have my assistant send it over today. Can't wait to see you. It'll be just like old times."

"Yeah, it'll be great," Daniel said with as much sincerity as he could muster. Thankfully the call ended. He immediately put the conversation out of his mind and tried to go back to work. He had more important things to do than think about the assholes from high school.

"I'M GOING home for the day," Joanne said, breaking Daniel's concentration. He had lost track of the time again and hadn't realized he'd been working for hours. "I checked, and everyone is happy and no one is waiting on you." That was the sign of a successful day. "I forwarded your reunion e-mail to your standard one here, and you can look at it. I went ahead and put it on your calendar and made a reservation at the Plaza for that weekend so you can stay where your classmates are. I can cancel it if you'd like."

"I never said I was going to go," Daniel said, and she rolled her eyes.

"It's your fifteenth class reunion and you're a real success. Of course you're going to go."

Daniel shook his head. "I have no interest."

She came in and sat in one of the chairs. Daniel had built all of his business teams on the philosophy of openness and communication. So while he had an office because he dealt with private matters, his door was almost always open and his walls were glass. He had nothing to hide from the people on his team, and he expected the same from them. That also meant people tended to offer advice and speak their mind—sometimes whether Daniel wanted it or not.

"I didn't know you went to Lipton. That must have been exciting." She looked at him strangely. "I always thought your background was more… humble than that."

Daniel closed the lid on his laptop. "It is." He didn't want to get into that right now. There were some things he felt were private, and Joanne was skating very close to them at the moment. "I was on a scholarship."

She watched him closely for a minute. "I see."

Sometimes she scared the hell out of him with the way she could grasp the deeper meaning from just a few words. He should have said nothing at all.

"What does that look mean?"

"Nothing. Just that no matter what happened then, you're extremely successful and you can hold your own with those people."

Daniel leaned forward. "Those people…," he began, and swore at himself for taking the bait, "they only cared about where their parents came from. They were all old money, as though that made them better than everyone else. It wasn't about what you did or how well you did, but how far back you could trace the money in your family. There was a Vanderbilt relative in my class, for God's sake. And the parents were just as shallow as their children. Yes, I got a good education that gave me a good start into college and beyond, but it was hell, and the last thing I want to do is—"

Joanne scoffed. "There is only one thing that gets you pissy like this, and that's when you say you don't want to do something but you really do. You'd love nothing more than to go to that reunion, sitting at the top of the heap in every way possible. You want to go to this shindig real bad and show them just the kind of success you've become."

"Yeah." He rolled his eyes. "These guys are not going to be impressed or care that I have a big Internet company. They have more money than you can imagine."

"Like I was going to say. You're a success, but you have to go with someone."

"God, I haven't had the time to date anyone in, what? Three years?"

"Three years, two months, and twelve days, but who's counting? The thing is, you need to find someone so you can go to this reunion and hold your head high. Hell, you can take the place by storm." Joanne came around his desk, opened the lid of his computer, and brought up a web page. "This is exactly what you need."

"A matchmaker?" Daniel figured he'd finally sent Joanne around the bend. Maybe she needed a vacation.

"Why not? This is a discreet, expensive agency with high-class clientele. Lots of guys like you spend all their time working and building their dream, and they forget about a personal life and have no time to date. So the old-fashioned matchmaker has a modern application. I'll call them and make an appointment for you. They'll talk to you and get the ball rolling." She worked through the website. "They don't discriminate and work with men and women, gay or straight. They even have aristocrats." She turned the computer so Daniel could see the screen. "Here's Count Gregor of Villovia and his new wife, Diana. Think about it. A title would certainly burn their asses at the reunion."

Daniel groaned. "I suppose you aren't going to leave me alone until I agree to do this." He could just see the puppy-dog looks he'd get until he complied—like the one she was giving him now. "Sometimes I really hate you."

"I know. But who else is going to look after you?" She grinned, knowing she'd won. Daniel often wondered who the hell the boss was in their relationship. "I'll take care of everything in the morning." She was too damned happy about this. "I know you aren't really interested, but I don't want you alone for the rest of your life." She stood and walked to the doorway, then motioned to the office. "What you've built is amazing, but you need someone to share it with."

"Fine. I'll agree to do this, but you have to leave me alone about it, and under no circumstances are you to tell anyone about it at all. Not a soul in the office, and certainly not my sister." He glowered at her. "Or Marty, for that matter. Your husband might blab at one of the parties. This is one of those things that you keep to yourself, or I'll start talking about the places you got a sunburn at the last company retreat."

"You wouldn't dare," she countered, clearly a little nervous. Of course, Daniel would never say anything. Joanne knew too many of his own secrets.

"You keep quiet, and I'll do the same."

"Deal." She turned and left, and Daniel wondered once again what he'd just agreed to. He went back to work because it never stopped, and staying on top of things was the only way he was going to help ensure his companies stayed ahead of the competition. And in the world of e-commerce, that was truly the name of the game.

"All right," Joanne said as she strode into his office a half hour later.

"I thought you were leaving."

"Yeah, right. I figured I better do this before you changed your mind and chickened out. I contacted the agency, and they had a cancellation, so you have an appointment set up for you tomorrow. They are very excited to work with you, and I already added them to your schedule. They will be here at two tomorrow afternoon, and I put them in the conference room near the entrance so they won't walk through the office. Now I'm going home." She left his office again to gather her things at her desk.

"Thank you… I think," Daniel called after her. He shook his head and figured it was time for him to go home too. He could work just as easily there and he was getting hungry. Daniel tried to remember if he had any food in the house. He didn't think so.

"I had groceries delivered today so you wouldn't starve," Joanne said as she walked in front of his office on her way out. "So please go home and relax for at least an hour tonight. There are plenty of things for sandwiches, and I ordered some nice salads that you'll like. No frozen dinners." She grinned to tell him she was done with her torment.

"What would I do without you?" Daniel heard her laugh grow softer as she got farther away. She was the closest to a real relationship he'd come in years. If he were straight and she weren't already married, there might have been something between them. Joanne was the kind of person he could really love having in his life. Self-assured, organized, caring, thoughtful, funny, and didn't take crap from anyone, including him.

DANIEL SAT in the conference room a little before two the following afternoon, second-guessing this whole damn thing. Sure, he wanted someone special to go to the reunion with, and it would be great if he could out-blueblood the supposed bluebloods he'd gone to school with, but was that worth all this bother? He always figured that he'd find someone on his own eventually.

"Daniel," Joanne said gently from behind him, and he finished what he'd been working on and closed the lid of his laptop. "This is Valerie Worth. She's the director and founder of Perfect Mates."

Daniel took in the stunning raven-haired woman with perfect makeup and clothes that would make any straight man take notice from a hundred feet away. This was a woman designed to get attention, and she certainly did.

"It's a pleasure to meet you." Daniel shook her hand, surprised by her firm, strong grip. He liked that.

"The pleasure is all mine." Her smile was a hundred watts, but genuine and professional.

Joanne left and closed the door as Daniel motioned her to a seat.

"I was pleased to get the call from your office yesterday, and surprised. You've been on my radar for a while, and I hoped you'd contact us."

"Excuse me?" Daniel was shocked beyond belief.

"I know who the most eligible men are in this town, and you are definitely one of them." She looked him in the eye as she spoke, and Daniel felt more uncomfortable by the second. "I want to get to know the kind of man you are. I'm not going to be asking you a bunch of bullshit questions about the type of person you want—"

"Man I want," Daniel clarified, hoping she truly understood same-sex pairings.

Valerie didn't bat an eyelash. "Good. That answers that question. Most people have no clue what kind of person they really want. When I ask, I usually get some bullshit answer about the perfect person, and it means nothing because Prince Charming isn't out there, even for me. Thank God, because he would be too perfect to live with."

"All right. Then what do you want to know?" He expected her to get out a notebook, but her gaze didn't waver from him.

"Tell me about yourself. Where did you go to school?"

"I went to Lipton Prep on scholarship, and from there, Columbia. I worked hard the entire time while the other students played and partied. I was on a scholarship, and if my grades suffered, I was out, and I couldn't have that."

She seemed to sense that he'd said all he was going to at that point. "What about your family?"

"My sister and I were raised by our mother. My father was in the military and was killed shortly after my sister was born. He was on some classified mission that no one will talk about even today.

My mother mourned him until the day she died and did her best to raise the both of us alone. She had Dad's benefits and worked hard. Mom died when I was a junior and Regina was a freshman in college. We helped each other get through it, but after that point, we had to rely on ourselves and each other."

"So you are 100 percent a self-made man." She smiled again. "I love those clients. They are used to hard work and dedication because, contrary to popular belief, finding someone to spend the rest of your life with is hard work." She paused, and when Daniel simply nodded, she continued. "Where did you grow up?"

"East Texas. But Mom was determined that we were going to get out. So she sent us to schools out east. Regina finished high school in Beaumont, and as I said, I went to Lipton. Mom worked tirelessly to make sure we both got college scholarships. Regina went to Mount Holyoke. I worked for other people for a few years and then started my first online business. It did okay, and I sold it and used the proceeds to start West Coast Couture with my sister as the initial product designer. She now has her own label and supervises the design department for the site. I started Kick in the Pants eighteen months ago, and it's been a ride and a half." Daniel glanced at Valerie's footwear and smiled.

"Yes. These are your boots. I used your custom-fit feature, and they are among my favorite pairs."

Daniel loved happy customers. "Among?"

"I have three pairs of your boots and love them all. They feel like I'm wearing gloves." She smiled brightly. "What sort of relationships have you had in the past?"

"I'm assuming you don't mean one-night stands and stupid things done when I was too young to know better."

"Yes."

"When have I had time? I'm no virgin, but I haven't had a real boyfriend since college, and that didn't work out so well."

"Why not?" She leaned forward. "Tell me about it."

"His name was Theodore, and he was the youngest son of a Manhattan real estate dynasty. His father was and is a power in this town, and when we started dating, Theo was always careful with how much we were seen together."

"Was he in the closet?"

"I think I could have dealt with that. Well, maybe in a way." Daniel started to fidget and he stilled his hands. He hated when anyone saw him do that. It showed weakness, and he had vowed years ago never to let anyone see him as weak again. "See, he'd told his parents he was gay. Not that he was dating a kid from the wrong side of the tracks. His parents took one look at me, listened to my accent, and wanted nothing more to do with me. They saw their darling Theodore as settling down with another Upper East Side gay, having pretentious children, and looking exactly the way they did. I thought Theo would stand up to them—we'd been dating for three months and I thought he cared for me. He said he did, but not enough to give up their money."

"So they weren't phobes, just snobs."

Daniel was growing to like Valerie. "Exactly. He dropped me faster than you can say trust fund. After that, I didn't try dating. I worked and made myself a success." He knew it was in part so he could rub the assholes' faces in it someday.

"Okay," Valerie said. "What else do you want me to know?"

"Any guy you might think I'd be interested in better be smart, have a backbone, and not be afraid of hard work. I'll steamroll over him otherwise. As far as looks, I don't care. Beauty is only skin-deep, but ugly goes clear through to the bone."

"Noted." She still hadn't written a thing down. "How about money?"

"I've got plenty of that, but send me a gold digger and I'll sniff him out and send his ass packing quicker than a Texas twister. I worked hard for what I have, and I won't be taken advantage of. I'm not stingy, but I'm not stupid either. And it would be awesome if he has an interesting family. I don't have any other than my sister." Daniel leaned back in his chair. "What else do you want to know?"

"I think I have a pretty good picture of the type of guy you are. So I think I can find some men who'll catch your interest." She leaned forward once again. "How are you on dates?"

Daniel shrugged. "Normal, I guess. I suppose I'd like to meet a guy for dinner. I don't do clubs. People are drinking and get out of control. I don't like to be around people who do stupid things. I've already had enough of that in prep school and college. I'm thirty-three, not twenty-one. So someone with some life experience, maturity—even an older man—would be fine. Some club kid most definitely would not."

"Okay, then." Valerie finally opened the bag she'd carried with her and brought out some documentation. She went through the fees she charged for her services and reviewed how they would be billed. "I only guarantee that we will find people for you, and I want to make you happy."

Daniel looked over the agreement and signed it. Then he wrote her a check as a deposit and handed it to her.

"Before I forget, your assistant said you had a class reunion coming up."

"Yes, from Lipton. Fifteen years. A date would be nice, but—"

"I won't promise anything, but let's see what we can do." Valerie put the agreement back in her case and gave Daniel a copy. She stood gracefully, and Daniel followed suit. She shook his hand one more time and then left the conference room as statuesquely as anyone Daniel had ever seen.

Joanne was there to meet her, and Daniel assumed she escorted her out before returning to his office, as excited as a kitten with a ball of yarn. "So how did it go?"

"Fine."

"What's the next step?"

Daniel grinned evilly. "I take it she wouldn't tell you anything." He had noticed a confidentiality statement in the agreement. "We'll see where it goes from here. Now I have some work to do, and I think you do as well." He turned back to his computer and ignored Joanne's no doubt pissed-off glare.

THE OFFICE was emptying out at the end of what turned out to be an amazing afternoon. They had had a top sales day so far, and it showed no signs of slowing. One of the afternoon talk show guests, the latest sensation, had been asked about her boots, and she'd said she'd gotten them at Kick in the Pants. Since that moment, sales had taken off. Daniel had his PR people on the phone with her agents, and they were going to talk about her acting as a spokesperson for the line.

He said good night to people as they left and stopped by the IT department to make sure the systems were functioning under the load. All he got were grins, and then the guys went back to their keyboards.

"It's all cool, Daniel," Toby, the head of IT, told him, and then they continued on. Most of the people dressed business casual in the office, but it was always obvious who worked in IT. Superhero T-shirts, jeans, and old tennis shoes were the norm here. And Daniel was grateful for each and every one of these guys.

"Buy everyone dinner," Daniel said, passing Toby some money. "Make it a good one."

"Thanks. We're going to stay so when things slow down, we can add another server to the array and boost our capabilities. We don't need it now, but we will, and it's better to get the capacity while we can."

"Do what you have to…."

Toby waved a hand. "Don't worry. The suite will stay up. We've done this three times before with no issue." He smiled, and the guys waved as Daniel left the department, their chatter about bytes and processors more than Daniel could follow.

He decided it was time for him to go home. He'd take his computer and work from there. As he packed up his things, his private cell phone rang. Daniel answered it, hoping Regina was okay. Very few people had that number.

"Daniel, it's Valerie at Perfect Mates. I apologize for calling so late, but I found someone I'd like you to meet. He's in the country for a week on business. And I think he's someone who might interest you."

"Oh? Where's he from?"

"His name is Robert. He's a barrister from England, and he has a client with business here. This is his first time in the States." She sounded different than she had in the office, and Daniel couldn't quite place why. "He's a new client with us. I'll text you over a picture of him. I think Robert has the potential to be a match for you. If you're okay with having dinner, I'll call in a favor and get you reservations."

"Tonight? Isn't that short notice?"

"He's here for the week. Sometimes you have to be willing to take opportunities when they present themselves. All I'm offering is dinner."

"Okay," Daniel agreed. "Is this kind of thing normal?"

"Goodness, no," Valerie chuckled richly. "But it isn't often that I get this kind of feeling about clients either. I met with him an hour after I left you, and I got the impression the two of you might be right. Call it intuition or whatever. But I've been in this business long enough to not discount this kind of thing."

Daniel checked his watch. It was still before six, and a lonely evening with his computer and his butt on his fancy leather sofa loomed ahead of him. "All right. I need to go home and change. Make the reservation and I'll meet Robert."

"Good. I'll text you the details and a picture of him."

She said good-bye, and Daniel wasn't sure what he'd gotten himself into. When he'd let Joanne sign him up, he thought he'd have to wait days, not a few hours. Now he'd be having dinner with some man from England. It beat eating alone again, and maybe he'd have some fun. It wasn't like he had to see Robert again if things didn't work out. Daniel called his car service, and they had someone waiting for him when he got downstairs.

He was preoccupied during the ride home and couldn't get out of the car and up to his small apartment fast enough. Real estate in New York was out of sight, so Daniel lived in a nice, somewhat small place toward downtown. It wasn't huge by any standard, but he had a nice view and it was enough for him. At least the building was secure.

Daniel set his computer on his small table and opened it, then cleaned up and changed clothes between waiting for reports to come in. He finished dressing as his phone dinged with a message that he had a reservation for two at the Four Seasons, under Daniel's name, for seven thirty. She also included the photograph, and Daniel had to admit Robert was handsome. His skin was light, but he had expressive eyes and wavy, dark hair. If this was a recent photo, Robert was good-looking enough that Daniel forgot about his work for a few minutes, staring at the picture for longer than necessary.

He acknowledged the message and thanked Valerie. Then he finished getting dressed and made sure the reports were ready for him to review later. He phoned the car service to let them know where he was going and when he wanted to be picked up. And at seven thirty almost on the dot, he stepped out of the car and into the hotel, heading right to the restaurant, where he nearly bumped into Robert as he approached the hostess desk.

He was even more stunning in person.

"You have to be Robert. Daniel Fabian."

"Yes, Robert Morton. Nice to meet you, Daniel."

They shook hands, and the hostess approached, wearing a red dress that might have been one size too small from the way she was poured into it. "Right this way, sir," she purred and led them into the luxuriously appointed restaurant that glowed with gold and rich flowers and glittered with crystal chandeliers. Valerie certainly knew the restaurant to choose to impress.

Daniel motioned for Robert to go ahead of him, remembering the manners Mother had drilled into his head. She had been huge on education and acting properly at all times. Daniel had to admit that some of those lessons had gone by the wayside over the years, but he was thankful he remembered them now. They sat at a table near windows decorated to exude opulence.

"What brings you to New York?" Daniel asked once they were both seated.

Of course, their server appeared at the table as if by magic, placed their napkins on their laps, and presented the menus with a flourish. He briefly explained the menu and took their cocktail orders before leaving.

"This is my first visit," Robert began. "I...." He looked around and shook his head a little.

"Valerie explained that you were a barrister. So I know you usually argue in front of the courts. At least that's what your title implies." He loved Robert's accent and the warmth in his voice.

"Yes... well... my firm is one that usually handles smaller cases for people in trouble." Robert seemed uncomfortable. "When I finished reading for law, I really wanted to help people, so some friends and I opened a practice that specialized in the legal needs of everyday folks. Part of our cases are taken for free because it's what needs to happen." Robert looked around the restaurant. "I don't eat in places like this. It's...."

Daniel took a deep breath. This wasn't quite what he'd been expecting, but that wasn't to say he was disappointed. "I think I'm a little confused."

The server brought their drinks and left once again, leaving them to talk.

"You're confused? In the last six weeks, my life has been turned on its ear. I'm here in New York to help a client negotiate an oil purchase deal. I've done things like that on a smaller scale. But now I have clients searching me out, and the firm is suddenly very popular with clients that would never have looked at us twice before."

"Was that something you wanted?" Daniel asked, watching Robert closely. He wasn't sure where this conversation was going, but it had caught his interest.

"It's fine, and good for the firm." Robert seemed to stutter like he wasn't sure where he wanted the conversation to go. "What about you? What do you do?"

"I started the West Coast Couture website five years ago, and my latest venture is Kick in the Pants. We sell boots of all kinds."

Robert looked at him blankly, and Daniel wasn't sure if that was good or not. Robert clearly had no clue about his businesses, which meant he wasn't sitting across the table trying to figure out how much he was worth.

"I'm not much of a shopper, and it's difficult and expensive to shop at American sites and get the goods shipped to us."

"I understand that. I'm currently working to set up a division in Great Britain that could handle those sorts of things. We have a large number of European customers and there are a number of complexities, but we'll work through them for our clients."

Robert nodded but seemed a little preoccupied. If the entire evening went like this, things were going to be difficult. Daniel was starting to think it would be best to eat as quickly as possible and then go home and chalk this evening up to a learning experience. After all, did he really think the first date he went on in five years was going to set off fireworks?

"What sort of boots do you sell? Are they only cowboy boots?" Robert paused, his eyes widening in surprise. "I'm sorry. I shouldn't assume, but I guess from your accent and…." Robert blushed adorably. Daniel had to admit it was a good color on him, and Robert was more handsome in person than the photo he'd been sent.

"We sell all kinds, in many styles, for men, women, and children. Our latest innovation is a process so everyone can have custom boots." Daniel leaned forward a little. "A great-fitting pair of boots can be an almost sublime experience. They hug your foot in just the right way, don't rub, and can feel like a part of your foot. Quite frankly, I want every pair we sell to be every buyer's favorite footwear. So we developed a way to scan the customer's feet and can have boots custom-made for them. They're a little more expensive than ready-to-wear boots, which we offer as well, but they always fit perfectly."

"That seems like such a no-brainer. Why hasn't anyone done it before?"

"It wasn't the scanning part. That can be done using a smartphone app or a tablet. It was developing the ability to take the data points—like with a fingerprint, but with more points—and creating the machines that can convert the scan into the actual boots. We launched it a few months ago for a limited number of boot models, and it's been a runaway success. We've added more styles and have plans to continue adding them. Maybe we could get you a pair while you're here."

"Possibly."

Robert seemed very reserved, and Daniel wondered if that was a British thing or if it was something else. He needed something to talk about and wasn't quite sure what it was. When he saw the server and caught his eye, the server approached and they placed their orders. It gave them something to do for a few minutes anyway.

"Have you ever used a matchmaker before?" Daniel asked once the server was gone.

"Goodness, no. You?"

"Nope." Daniel smiled. "Did you get talked into it too?"

That got him a smile, and damned if Robert's expression didn't brighten and his eyes light up. This was a man made for smiling, and he definitely needed to do it more often. His teeth were perfect, and little lines extended up his cheeks and to his eyes.

"My mother," Robert said, his accent becoming more pronounced, and Daniel thought that sexy as well. "You?"

"My assistant. I think she tries to mother me as much as she can. Joanne thinks I need to get out and meet more people." That was true enough, and it spared him from talking about what really prompted him to do this. In his mind it made Daniel look like a loser. "I can't argue with her. This is my first… date… in a number of years. I was always too busy working."

"Me too. It's just my mother and me now, so between the practice and looking after her, I don't have much time. I noticed you didn't mention family."

Daniel nodded. "It's just my sister and me now. Regina is based here in New York, but she travels a lot. She's starting her own fashion house and is taking Europe by storm at the moment."

"Where does she design?"

"Regina is one of those people who works anywhere and everywhere. She would be lost without her computers. She's here part of the year, where she pretty much holes up and works, and then she travels to promote and show her work. It keeps her very busy."

"So you don't get to see her that often?" Robert's expression warmed.

"No. Not nearly as much as I'd like. But she has her life. She's been dating a man here in New York. He's the director of a technology firm, and the two of them seem to get along. I don't know how their relationship can last with Regina away as much as she is, but they seem to make it work and she's happy. That's all I want for her."

"I'm an only child." Robert paused. "My mum had troubles having children. She lost two before she had me, and after that, she didn't try anymore. My father passed away six years ago, and since then it's just been my mother and me. She still lives in the same cottage and takes care of herself, but I know she misses him to this day. They were a real love match, and she…. Well, theirs is a story out of a romance novel, I suppose."

"How so?" Daniel was more than a little intrigued, and when their first courses arrived, he was so intent on Robert's story, he barely noticed.

"My mother's family had position and authority."

Daniel let that digest. "Like country gentry?"

"Something like that," Robert said, lightly shaking his head. "She fell in love with my father, and the family disowned her. Her family was pretty terrible about it. But to my mother, my dad was worth it. I never heard a cross word between them, and when things were tough, they banded together and didn't snipe at each other."

Daniel had never had that kind of relationship in his life. He'd always assumed that his mother and father loved each other very much—that's what his mother had told him anyway, and he believed it. But Daniel supposed it would be different to actually be able to see and experience the love between his parents. If he had, maybe he would have put a higher priority on finding that in his own life.

"I'm sorry you lost your dad."

"Part of what he did was make furniture. I always believed he was an artisan at heart. He worked hard all his life, and my mum's cottage is filled with things he made. She says it helps her feel close to him."

"My father died when I was six." Daniel searched his memory as he took a bite of radicchio salad. "I remember my dad taking me to the zoo in Dallas. I remember it because my dad had said it was supposed to rain, so he filled the car with umbrellas and raincoats because Mom insisted we be prepared. When it rains in Dallas, it pours something awful. But that day the sun shone, and my dad lifted me onto his shoulders. I got to see the giraffes and monkeys from high up. In my memory it seems like I could touch the sky." Daniel closed his eyes for a second. "I remember reaching down to stroke my dad's cheek, and it was rough. I told him he had sandpaper cheeks, and he laughed and took me to see the bears." Unfortunately, Daniel had very few memories of his father that had stuck with him over the years. His mother had some photo albums, and he used to look through them so much that sometimes he wasn't sure which were real memories or just his mother's stories planted so deeply into his mind that it was sometimes hard to tell them apart.

"That sounds like a good memory to have."

Daniel nodded and returned to his salad. "How about we talk about something livelier? What's life like in London?"

"I wouldn't really know. I live in Smithford. It's a small community, mostly farming and agriculture, in the Midlands and slightly to the west near Cornwall. It's a very nice place, and families have lived there for many generations. There are plenty of animals, and when I drive, I'm more likely to be stuck behind a hay wagon than anything else. It's where I grew up and also where I have the bulk of my practice."

"Then, if it isn't prying, why are you suddenly getting these large clients who want you to come here for them? Not that the place doesn't sound nice—it seems quiet. I had a friend growing up who lived on a farm, and I used to go out to visit all the time. Randy and I used to get in so much trouble."

Robert sat back and chuckled deeply. It was the first time that Daniel had seen him relaxed. "I had a friend like that. The entire village used to live in fear of us. Liam was a real prankster. He used to tie ribbons to one of the cows and then let it loose in the village. The poor thing would run through the main street looking like some parade float run amok. One time he pasted a horn in the center of one of the goats' foreheads and got one of the kids to call into the newspaper to say that they'd discovered a unicorn."

"No one would believe that," Daniel said.

"Of course not. But it made it into the paper anyway. He'd dyed the poor thing rainbow colors. It looked like some demented My Little Pony." Robert laughed outright, leaning forward so he wouldn't make too much noise.

Daniel tried not to make a scene and failed completely. The image of a rainbow goat in a field with a horn in the middle of its head was too dang much. "It feels good to laugh."

"I take it you don't do that very often." Robert brought his napkin to his lips and then dabbed his eyes before returning it to his lap.

"I haven't thought about it, but I probably don't as much as I should." There wasn't a lot to laugh about in his life, if he thought about it, and there hadn't been in some time. "My life is work, my sister, and more work. I don't think I've taken much time for anything else."

Their main courses arrived, and the conversation grew quiet while each artfully prepared plate was set in front of them with a flourish. Daniel hadn't known how hungry he was until the savory aroma of his trout in brown butter wafted up to him. He had to stop himself from eating as quickly as he would at home and savor each and every bite.

"If it's not prying, do you think there would be time in your life if you were to meet someone you were interested in?" Robert asked.

Daniel hadn't really given that too much thought. Whirlwind Joanne had arranged things so quickly that he hadn't even had a chance to think about what actually meeting someone would mean to his life. "You know, I think it would be nice to have someone to go to dinner with and do things with." He didn't mention how amazing it would be to have someone like Robert in his bed every night. He took a bite to look away, and an image came to mind of him in bed, sweaty and sated, smiling as he turned to the man in his bed, who looked a lot like Robert, and saw him smile back. His imaginary Robert leaned closer, kissed him, and then whispered something funny in his ear. "Someone to talk with," he said almost in a whisper that might not have been able to be heard over the other conversation in the restaurant. "I bet you're busy as well."

"Yes. The practice keeps me busy...."

Robert paused once again, and Daniel knew Robert was skirting around something he wasn't sure he wanted to talk about. Daniel had been in business long enough and worked enough deals to know when someone was being evasive. He continued eating and let Robert work through whatever was worrying him. As he watched him, he could almost see the wheels turning. Daniel continued enjoying his trout, waiting Robert out.

"Things in my life really changed six weeks ago." Robert set down his fork. "My uncle passed away and left me as his heir. Well, he didn't have much of a choice. Much of the estate is entailed, which means that the terms of inheritance had already been set down and he couldn't change it."

Daniel met Robert's gaze. "So does that mean you have a title?"

"Yes. Officially I'm the Earl of Hantford. But I don't feel like an earl. It's the title that has brought me the extra business over the past weeks." He picked up his fork again. "Before I had the title, I was another barrister in a small firm in the Midlands, but as soon as I inherited, I somehow became an expert in the law who everyone wants to deal with."

"Did you get a country estate, like Downton Abbey?" Daniel had to ask, but the shudder told him that was a sore subject.

"Yes, I have an estate, but it's nothing like Downton Abbey— at least the real building anyway. The place is outdated, needs a new roof, plumbing, electrics, and God knows what else. I also received a house in London that needs the same kind of work. I'm trying to figure out what I'm going to do with the pile."

"Fix it up and open it to the public," Daniel offered.

"It's going to take millions of pounds to do that, and there isn't enough income to support a loan. I'll probably sell the London house. It has value because it's in a highly desirable location, and someone will want to do the work because the interior hasn't been messed up. But that's only going to get me started on what needs to be done at Ashton Park." Robert groaned. "On top of that, I have tenants who rent homes and cottages from the estate, and I need to think of them. There are thousands of acres, but much of it has been left fallow or overgrown. There used to be a park around the estate, but much of that has gone wild over the years. Everywhere I look, there's more work to be done—work that costs ungodly amounts of money. So I take the cases that have come my way because they pay very well, but they don't make me particularly happy." Robert returned his attention to his dinner. "I shouldn't complain. I have more than most. But I was happy before this landed on my shoulders."

Daniel was a little floored. His mind was already running through possible business scenarios. "You said the area was farming country? So if you have so much land, put it to use. With modern methods, it isn't like it was when the estate was prospering. You could get one man and some equipment and make part of the land pay. Either that or you could graze cattle or sheep. Those have been raised in the UK for centuries. From what I understand, food prices are higher over there, so you might be able to make some money, especially if you found a product you could specialize in, like that Swiss butter that is so prized." Once he started talking, Daniel's idea flowed freely. At first he wasn't sure if Robert wanted to hear what he had to say, but Robert leaned a little closer while he ate, his full attention on Daniel. "Aren't there estates that have made a go of it?"

"Yes. Many of them exist on tourism. There is one that has a race course and an annual racing event. But that isn't possible for us."

"No. But what is? Have you talked to a business manager? Think of hiring someone who could look at what you have and develop ideas that you could implement. If you have resources, which you do, then all you need is to think about how they can be converted into a regular income. Once you have that, you use the money to repair and develop the property, which in turn brings in more income."

"You make it sound so simple. I'm a barrister, not a business manager. These kind of ideas don't come easily to me." The frustration was clear in Robert's voice. "But I think your advice is good, and I'll look into finding a man of business who can work with me on some ideas. I just have to figure out how I'm going to pay him."

"Do you have pictures of the place?"

Robert pulled out his phone, brought up the picture app, and flipped through before handing over the phone.

"That looks like something out of a movie," Daniel said, looking at the view down the drive, up to the front of the massive house. "I love the two towers in front. They give it a historic feel. Like it's been there forever."

"Ten generations. That's the problem. My uncle didn't do his duty. See, the way I look at it, I'm only the caretaker of the place, and I need to leave it in better condition than I found it. Which shouldn't be hard, considering—"

"Do you have someone to leave it to? I'm assuming your uncle didn't if the property went to you."

"That's yet another hurdle I have to figure a way around. I'm looking into it. I believe that I could adopt a child, and as long as I did it with full legality and appoint them as the heir, then I can leave it to my child. So that issue is covered, I think. Still, I want there to be something worth leaving." Now that he'd opened the lid on the jar, Robert seemed content talking about his situation.

Time seemed to fly from then on. The server brought the dessert selections, but they both passed. Daniel was full, and it wasn't as though he needed the extra calories. They both had coffee, and then Daniel paid the bill and they got up to leave. "You said this your first time in New York?"

"It is, actually." Robert hesitated. "I was wondering if I could see you again while I'm here."

"That would be great." Daniel pulled out his wallet and handed Robert one of his seldom-used personal cards. He'd always wondered why Joanne had them made up, though now he was grateful. "I'd love to see you again." He checked his calendar for later in the week. "Are you working on Saturday?"

"I'll probably have some things to catch up on, but I don't have meetings or anything."

Daniel didn't have any either, so he blocked out the entire day. "Then I'll meet you for bagels at ten, and I can show you the city if you like."

"Are you sure?"

"Yeah. It's like a staycation. New Yorkers never do any of the touristy things that surround us. So make a list of what interests you and send it over. I have contacts, so I can get tickets or pave the way if necessary." He was tickled pink, and for the first time in recent memory, he found he was looking forward to a weekend. Usually weekends were just his time to catch up on the things he didn't get done during the week.

"If you're sure that wouldn't mess things up for you."

Daniel chuckled as they left the hotel and stepped out onto the sidewalk. He'd neglected to send a message to his car service, so he did that now. "My assistant, Joanne, will probably do a happy dance and wonder if the world stopped spinning when I tell her I'm taking the day off. But that's what I'm going to do. I have a hard time letting others take on things, so it's time I let go and step back a little. It will be good."

"So ten on Saturday," Robert agreed, and Daniel's phone chimed with a message. "Now you have my number. I put in the message how to call me from here, so that will work."

Daniel's car pulled up under the portico, and he stepped forward. "Can I take you anywhere?"

Robert seemed to consider, then nodded, and Daniel smiled.

The driver held the door and Daniel waited for Robert to get inside. Then he settled on the backseat next to him, closed the door, and the car started forward. Robert must have already told the driver where to take him because the driver headed out as though he knew where to go. Daniel didn't stop him because he was too wrapped up in Robert's hazel eyes to think about anything else.

They pulled up to the Marriott near Times Square and made the turn into the passage through the middle of the ground floor of the building. It was filled with cars, so they just managed to get off the street. Robert reached for the door, but Daniel placed a hand on his shoulder, stopping him. When Robert turned back, Daniel leaned in and saw Robert do the same.

The car lurched forward and Daniel's balance left him for a few seconds. Robert caught him, but not before Daniel leaned on top of him, his lips mere inches from Robert's. Daniel closed the gap between them. Robert tasted savory and warm, and damned if he didn't know how to kiss. His lips were firm, moist, and he returned the kiss, gently placing his hand on Daniel's shoulder. When he backed away, Daniel blinked a few times to make sure he'd actually kissed Robert and to clear the cloud of want from his head. Robert definitely tasted like potential.

The driver pulled the car over, got out, and opened the door on Robert's side, which brought an end to the mini fantasy playing in Daniel's head.

"I'll see you Saturday." Robert smiled and then got out of the car.

The door closed behind him, and Daniel watched through the window as Robert entered the hotel. After a minute, the car started forward once again, taking him back to his condo… alone.

CHAPTER 3

"YOUR DATE went well?" Valerie asked when Robert called her in the morning. She seemed too chipper for eight o'clock, but Robert was still adjusting to the time in New York. His body didn't know when to sleep or wake yet.

"Very well. Daniel was very nice, and we talked about things I hadn't expected to." That was the best way to describe it. Robert still wondered if he'd said too much, but Daniel had seemed to take it in stride. Most people fixated on the title and what came with it. Robert wasn't interested in impressing people because of what he'd inherited. He was more interested in being appreciated and respected for what he did.

"Robert," Valerie said, caution clear in her voice. "It was a first date. I told you to keep the conversation light and general. People don't want to get into heavy personal things. It makes them uncomfortable."

"Daniel and I had a nice date, and after a slow start, we talked about all kinds of things. He told me about himself, and I did the same. And we made another date for Saturday. We're going to have bagels, and then he's going to show me the sights." Robert grinned, grateful no one could see him. He was alone in a conference room, and his first meeting wasn't for an hour yet. "He kissed me good night."

"Wait a minute. Daniel is showing you the sights on Saturday?"

"He's taking a day off. He said he hadn't had one in years and it was time he did." Robert was actually starting to feel hopeful that this idea might just work out. Daniel was nice and he definitely had the money to help him. That had been why Robert had signed up for the dating service in the first place, to try to find a guy who would be willing to help him out in exchange for a title. That had been the plan, though already Robert was second-guessing himself. This was such a harebrained scheme, and Daniel had been nice, truly a good guy. Plus, Robert liked him.

"Very good. It does sound as though the two of you hit it off."

"Have you talked to Daniel?" Robert asked.

"Not yet. But I will sometime today. Just relax and look forward to Saturday. I'm here if you need anything."

"Daniel asked me to send him a list of things I'd like to do and he'd get tickets for anything we needed. He's a real nice guy."

"Good." Valerie cleared her throat. "Now comes the difficult part. Do you think there was a spark between you? When he kissed you, was there energy and excitement?"

Robert coughed and reached for the bottle of water on the table. He took a drink to settle his throat. Robert hadn't expected questions like that, but he probably should have. The matchmaking thing was new to him. Maybe it was his reserved nature.

"Yes," he answered simply. He wasn't going to give her any of the details.

"All right. I can tell you're uncomfortable. Call me if you need anything."

Valerie ended the call after Robert agreed, and he returned his mind to the tasks he needed to complete today and tomorrow before his next date.

DANIEL CALLED Friday afternoon to confirm that they were still on for Saturday.

"What did your assistant say when you took the day off?" Robert asked.

"I think the term 'over the moon' was invented for that occasion, as was 'gobsmacked.' She was definitely both. So I'll pick you up at your hotel at ten, and we can pretty much walk from there. The weather is supposed to be lovely. You didn't tell me what you wanted to do."

"Because I decided to let you do the choosing. You know the city best, and I thought it might be fun to go where the wind blew for a while. Is that okay?"

"It's perfect. We'll have breakfast and go from there."

Robert could almost see the smile form on Daniel's lips and his bright eyes shining. Last night when he hadn't been able to sleep right away, Robert had stared up at the ceiling, imagining his smile.

"I have some people waiting to see me, so I have to go. But I'll see you tomorrow morning."

Daniel hung up, and Robert finished getting ready for his day. Somehow he had to get his mind on the tasks at hand.

AT TEN Saturday morning, Robert was dressed and waiting for Daniel to arrive. A black car pulled in, Daniel got out and strode to where Robert stood, and the car pulled away. Daniel's jeans and a T-shirt made Robert felt a little overdressed with his slacks and a white oxford, but those were the most casual clothes he had.

"Good morning," Robert called, smiling.

"Good morning. My favorite bagel place isn't too far from here. It's just a few blocks."

"I wore comfortable shoes." Robert noticed that Daniel was in a pair of boots that looked butter-soft. "I have to get a pair of those while I'm here." He had meant to do it earlier, but work had pulled his mind in other directions.

"We can arrange for that," Daniel said as they left the hotel and turned west.

Robert followed along, spending much of his time looking up as building after building passed above him. It was a weird feeling, these canyons of brick, steel, and glass.

Daniel led him into a small shop on 39th that bustled with activity and smelled heavily of bread and baking. "Do you want me to order for you?"

"That would be great," Robert said as a table opened up, and he took a seat while Daniel got in line. He returned with two coffees and two wax envelopes, and placed one of each in front of each of them. "You remembered," Robert said as he sipped the coffee.

"You took a little cream at the restaurant. I had them add a little more because they have extrastrong coffee here." Daniel sipped from his own cup and then opened his envelope. The cream cheese burst from the bagels. "I got garlic and onion for both of us. I love the flavor, and I figured if we both had garlic breath, then neither of us would notice."

Robert took a bite, the bread a little chewy but bursting with flavor, cooled by the smooth cream cheese. "These are brilliant."

"I'm glad you like it."

They settled in to eat. It was a little too loud to carry on much conversation, with people coming and going the entire time. Robert didn't press and simply ate, trying to remember his manners and not wolf down his food.

"I always have to remember when I'm with other people not to eat too fast. Mostly at home, I eat at my desk where there's no one around to watch." He took a bite and felt cream cheese sticking to his cheek. He wiped his mouth, but Daniel reached over.

"You missed a spot," he said softly as their eyes met. Robert's pulse quickened slightly when he thought Daniel might kiss him, but he simply wiped his mouth with a soft touch. "There."

They finished their bagels, Daniel took care of the trash, and then they left, carrying their coffee as they walked.

"Where are we headed?"

They stopped on the sidewalk and Daniel turned to him. "Downtown is that way. We can go to the Statue of Liberty, Wall Street, the Brooklyn Bridge, or uptown so we can walk through Central Park." Daniel waited for him to answer, and Robert looked both ways before heading uptown. "Good choice on a day like this. I thought we'd go over and walk up Fifth. There are things to see on the way."

"So how did a boy from Texas end up here in New York?" Robert asked as they walked.

"I went to prep school in upstate New York and then to Columbia University here in New York City. By the time I graduated, there wasn't much of a reason for me to go back. There were jobs here, and I was able to get a start. Then after I started the business, I found wonderful people here. This had become my home, so I stayed."

"Prep school? Like Eaton?" Robert asked.

"Only mine was Lipton. It's the American equivalent. But I was a scholarship kid, so...."

Robert nodded. "I know how that feels. I went to a school like that too. My mum said it was important, so she went to work so that I could go. I hated every minute of it, and after a year, I went to school closer to home."

"Yeah." Daniel sighed as they stopped at a street corner to wait for the light to change. "I never fit in, but Mom worked so hard and wanted me to have chances that she never had, so I stuck it out. It wasn't too bad, except that some of the kids made fun of me because I didn't have the latest clothes. I didn't go home to houses in the Hamptons or to cabins in the Adirondacks during the winter ski season." It was clear that Daniel had felt shut out by the other kids. "It changed somewhat when I went to college, but a lot of the other kids came from rich backgrounds and—" Daniel stopped when the light changed and they crossed the street. "So has your business been going well?"

"Nice change of subject." Not that Robert blamed Daniel. The topic had gotten much more serious than he'd intended. "Let's talk about something happier. So why did you call a matchmaker? I mean, you could have done things the old-fashioned way."

"I don't have much time to date, and it became easier to stay at home instead of making the effort after long days."

Robert looked at Daniel when they stopped at the next corner. "I can tell that's bollocks. I'm a barrister—I ferret out evasion for a living."

The light changed and they crossed the street with the flow of pedestrians. "Fine. Joanne talked me into it. I have a class reunion from Lipton coming up, and she didn't want me going alone. Those people are…. They're like the people who hire you because you're an earl. They don't care about your accomplishments as much as who you are or where you came from. Even as kids they were all worried about making the friends who would benefit them later. It was sickening." Daniel clenched his hands into fists.

"So you were looking for a date? Someone you could take to your reunion that would impress them. I bet an earl would do that." Robert grinned and got a matching one in return.

"Yes, it probably would. But I think we're getting ahead of ourselves."

Robert nodded his agreement, but on the inside, his heart pumped a little faster. He liked Daniel, but he wasn't going to rush into anything. Things might actually work out if he were careful.

They continued walking toward the park. "What's that?"

"The New York Public Library," Daniel said. "I used to spend a lot of time in there when I was a student. They have some amazing books." He motioned up the steps. "Let's go into the main reading room." He led the way up the stairs and into the library, through the foyer and up to the main reading room. "This room has been used in a lot of movies." Daniel looked up and Robert followed his gaze.

"It's stunning," Robert whispered. He saw a lot of stylistic similarities between this ceiling and the one in the library at Ashton Park, only this one had been cleaned and cared for, while his wasn't as big and was dingy and in need of some help.

"There are other collections that you can wander through if you like. But I like to come in here."

"We can do whatever you like." Robert was enjoying Daniel's company quite a bit, and it was becoming less and less about what they did and more about the fact that Daniel was sharing with him some of his favorite places.

Daniel showed him around a little more, and then they left and continued on up toward the park. The line of trees and green loomed closer and closer. "That's the Plaza Hotel. They're having our class reunion there. It's probably one of the most famous addresses in the city."

"Have you ever been there?"

Daniel shook his head.

"Why not? You could certainly afford to eat there if you wanted."

"I know. It's just that...." He turned away, and Robert wondered if he'd said something he shouldn't. "It still feels like I don't belong there. That's the domain of the people with more than money. They eat there and have their little power lunches and dinners. I could eat there too, but it isn't like I'd ever belong to their group. I was well and truly shut out in school, and I somehow doubt anything has really changed. Things like that don't."

Daniel turned, and Robert followed him to the corner, then across the street and into the park. "I love it here," Daniel said once they were under the canopy of the trees.

"It's beautiful."

"This is every New Yorker's backyard. The city is so built up that there is little private green space, so this is everyone's green space."

They continued walking along the tree-covered path. People sat on the benches that lined the way, some whiling away the hours and others having a family outing. A pair of children raced to a man, delight on their faces as he handed each an ice cream cone.

"How big is the park?"

"From 59th Street, which we just crossed, to 110th Street, and between 5th Avenue and Central Park West. So it's really the heart of the city." Daniel stopped and turned to him. "Do you like to boat? We can rent row boats on the lagoon, or there is a place to rent pedal boats to use on one of the lakes. The Metropolitan Museum is on this side the park, about halfway down. We can walk that way. We don't have to go inside, but Cleopatra's Needle is behind the building."

Robert followed, enjoying the peace and quiet. "Are you sure this is how you'd like to spend the day? I don't know, but it seems like you'd want something more active."

"Is that what you want?" Daniel asked. "This is New York. Everything you could imagine is here if you know where to look for it."

"I'm having a great time."

"So am I. I spend my days running a million miles an hour as a business adrenaline junkie with pressure galore. I have nearly a thousand people who work for me, so if I make a bad decision, then it affects all their lives. So I think a little downtime is what I needed." Daniel rolled his shoulders, and as he continued walking, Robert noticed that Daniel's arms swung a little more freely and his gait seemed less intense and more flowing as tension drained out of him.

They continued through the park past the zoo. "That's Bethesda Terrace and Fountain. The boathouse is over there." They walked to the dock, rented a boat, and then gradually made their way around the lake.

"It's been a long time since I've been on the water," Robert admitted, hoping he didn't get queasy. "The last time I didn't fare so well."

"What happened?"

"Gerald is a friend from college, and he got the bright idea to take a ferry to the continent. We were going to see some of the country. Anyway, the entire crossing I was at the rails, and I made him take the Channel Tunnel back because I refused to set foot on that ferry again."

"Well, I doubt there are going to be waves on this trip." Daniel continued rowing and then slowed so they could coast in the sunshine. "In the movies, this is where the boy and the girl look longingly into each other's eyes." He set the oars in their holders and carefully moved toward where Robert sat.

"Did you ever lie in a meadow and look up at the clouds to see the shapes?" Robert asked.

"Well, in Texas that really isn't the best of ideas. I tried once after I saw it in a movie, and I ended up getting bitten by fire ants. I ran back to the house, and Mom turned the hose on me to get them to stop stinging." Daniel quivered. "The dang things burn like heck, and I never tried it again."

"Well." Robert looked skyward. "There are no fire ants here unless they're really good swimmers." He chuckled. "My mum told me that she and my dad cloud-gazed on their first date. They weren't supposed to see each other, but they did anyway, and my dad took her on a picnic."

"I don't have a basket." Daniel carefully moved to sit next to Robert in the middle of the boat, and his warmth combined with the heat of the day to send beads of sweat rising on Robert's neck. "Maybe after this we can get something for an impromptu picnic. Look… there's a horse."

Robert smiled. "Yeah, and when it merges with that other cloud, it'll be an elephant. I love elephants. I used to watch *Babar* as a child and wish I could go there."

"There's an ice cream cone." Daniel grinned. "If I'm starting to see food in the clouds, then maybe we should think about lunch sooner rather than later."

Robert chuckled. "That's a hot dog, and over there is a trifle."

Daniel laughed, and Robert joined him, the boat rocking a little in their mirth and Robert not caring in the least. "And that over there is cotton candy…. I think you call it candy floss." Daniel was surely teasing. "I like the pink kind."

"I always loved the purple," Robert said, and they devolved into laughter once again. Daniel turned and leaned closer, catching Robert's gaze. He smiled, and the intensity that shone in Daniel's eyes drew Robert in, pulling him closer until Robert realized what was happening in the middle of the lake with hundreds of people looking on. "We shouldn't do this here."

Daniel blinked and turned away, blushing. "I got carried away. You seem to have that effect on me." He took the oars once again and rowed them around the lake and then back to the boat dock. "I don't know about you, but I worked up an appetite." Daniel led the way to one of the food carts that were everywhere in the park. He ordered two New York hotdogs with everything and got two bottles of water.

Robert wasn't quite sure what to make of the food, but he tried it when Daniel handed him the hot dog. "This is really good."

"It's a New York institution." Daniel took a bite. "We can go find somewhere to get a more substantial lunch, but you have to have one of these while you're here." He took another bite and then guzzled his water.

Suddenly ravenous, Robert finished his hot dog and drank his water. "Lead on."

Daniel took care of the trash, and they continued deeper into the park. "That's Belvedere Castle." Daniel pointed. "All of the lakes in the park are manmade. There were a few streams and things when the park was commissioned, and the water from those was used to make the lakes. Almost all the trees were planted as well."

"Is anything in the park according to nature?"

Daniel led him to a large rocky outcrop. "This is some of the exposed Manhattan bedrock, and do you see those lines? Those are from the glaciers ten thousand years ago. The marks are all over the park. It's this same rock that allows the city to grow upward because it's so hard."

"Is there anything you don't know?" Robert asked, starting to feel a little intimidated.

"Yeah, plenty. In school I developed a first-class memory. When I learn something, it stays until I need it." Daniel turned away and led them back the way they'd come. "Maybe it's time we got something real to eat. I could go inside the Plaza Hotel for the very first time."

"You choose anywhere you'd like to eat. It's more important to be comfortable with your surroundings than it is to eat in a fancy restaurant and feel out of place." Robert hurried to match Daniel's brisk steps and took his arm to slow him down. "I didn't mean to make you angry."

Daniel continued at a more moderate pace. "You didn't. It's just one of my buttons."

"They really did a number on you." Robert swallowed. He knew how cruel kids could be. He also knew what it felt like to be away from home and have the other kids act like the devil himself. Of course, he was supposed to have a stiff upper lip and take what they dished out so that when he got older, he could treat the younger kids the same way. It was part of the culture and supposed to make kids stronger. But Robert thought it stupid. "Let's go to the Plaza and say to hell with them." Robert grinned and leaned closer. "Let's have some fun with it." He walked faster and grinned to beat the band.

It took a while, but they emerged from the park, and Robert took the lead, walking across the street and into the Plaza.

"Where are you taking me?" Daniel asked.

"Where would you like to eat? The Palm Court sounds nice."

Daniel rolled his eyes. "We're never going to get a table. This place requires reservations to use the bathroom."

Robert smiled, and they made their way to the restaurant.

"Do you have a reservation?" the host asked from behind his little podium.

"No, I'm sorry." Robert stood tall and put on his best accent.

"Then I'm afraid I can't help you." He turned away, and Robert cleared his throat.

"Then I'd like to speak to the manager so you can explain to him how you turned away Robert Morton, the eleventh Earl of Hantford, and his companion, when they wished to eat in your establishment." Robert put on all the airs he possibly could and saw doubt creep into the host's features. He suddenly discovered a table that was available, and Robert and Daniel were ushered inside. "Snobby bugger," Robert said as soon as the host walked away.

"You did that so well." Daniel sat and looked all around, then up at the stained glass dome overhead.

"I don't like to, but sometimes it helps."

Daniel nodded. "You know, that's what the guys in my class used to do to me all the time. Whenever they wanted something, they'd haul out their titles or whatever else they thought made them important."

Robert swallowed hard. "I only wanted to make you happy. I wouldn't have said anything if I thought it was going to make you uncomfortable."

"I know." Daniel sighed. "It's part of how the world works. Sometimes you have to throw around a little muscle in order to get what you want."

Robert opened his menu and looked it over. The prices almost made him whistle. He'd muscled his way in here, but he really shouldn't be spending so much on a single lunch. He had other expenses and obligations that should come first. Still, he was here, and getting up to leave wasn't an option at this point. Robert chose what he wanted and then set his menu aside.

When one of the white-coated servers approached, they placed their orders, and thankfully Daniel seemed much happier.

"Is it what you thought it would be?" Robert asked.

Daniel shrugged and leaned over the table. "The service is nice and I expect the food to be very good, but it's just a restaurant like any other. Maybe fancier and with a better view." He glanced upward. "But it's still just a restaurant." He sat back stiffly, and Robert knew this was probably a mistake. Daniel was still nervous and looked like he felt out of place.

"Just relax. Like you said, it's only a restaurant." Robert smiled. "We could toss bread at each other if it would make you feel better."

"Robert," Daniel said, chuckling. "I can just see the headline: 'Earl starts food fight in Palm Court restaurant in the Plaza.' It would be all over the society pages."

"Yeah, I'd either get a reputation for being crazy or eccentric, and since I'm not old enough to be the latter, I guess they'd label me as crazy."

"Or a rebel." Daniel was grinning now, and the tension seemed to have left his body.

"Yeah. Can you see me in leather on a motorbike?" For some reason that was what came to mind when he thought about being a rebel, not tossing bread in the Plaza.

Daniel nodded and sipped his water. Their conversation lapsed, and Daniel continued looking around as though he was trying to puzzle something out. "Can I ask you something? You're only here for a week, and yet you hired a matchmaker here in New York to work with you. Why not hire one from London? I mean, that would make a lot more sense." He took another drink of water.

"That's one huge change of subject."

"Sorry, my brain does that sometimes."

Robert ran through the possibilities and decided that the truth was the best thing. "My mother signed me up when she learned that I was coming." God, that was so embarrassing. His mother.... Robert closed his eyes. "She had this idea that I should come over here, date wealthy American men, and hopefully find one that might be interested in coming back to England. Or at least...." He finished his water and his glass was refilled almost immediately. "This whole thing is so stupid, but I figured I'd go along with her, and then when nothing came of it...."

Daniel scratched the side of his head. "I think you're going to have to start at the beginning."

"Okay." He knew he had to be prepared for Daniel to simply get up and leave. "My mother is... in her own way... an old-school kind of person. She married my father, and when the family turned their back on her, she accepted it because it was the way things were done. So when I inherited the earldom and found out that the estate was nearly broke and needed money, her idea was to do what English nobility have always done when they needed an infusion of cash."

"Marry it," Daniel said levelly.

"Yes. So when I had to come to the US, my mother went ahead and contacted the matchmaker here. She wanted me to meet a rich American guy who would be willing to help me finance the restoration of Ashton Park. In return, my husband would get a title. Since the wife of an earl is a countess, she figured the husband of an earl would have the title of count. The whole idea is ridiculous." He sat up straighter. "I figured that since I was only here for a week, I'd have a date and things wouldn't work out, and then I'd go home and that would be the end of it. I'd puzzle out how to do what needed to be done—and you've given me some ideas…. I mean, the whole thing is absurd."

"Why?" Daniel asked. "You have a lot to offer someone."

Robert had half expected Daniel to be shocked or at least get angry. "Yeah, but the idea is so old-fashioned and—"

"As long as you're up front about what you expect and conduct things in an open manner…." Daniel paused, and Robert could almost see the wheels turning in his head. "It's a business arrangement of sorts. You get some money to start renovations on Ashton Park, and your husband would get an honorary title." Daniel smiled wryly. "I could just see the guys at my reunion if I was introduced as Daniel Fabian, Count of Hantford."

Robert didn't seize that idea too quickly because it would be most definitely rushing into things. But Daniel didn't seem to hate the thought outright. "That would certainly make them stand up and take notice."

"It would frost their asses no end." Daniel grinned almost evilly. "Would the man you marry have to live in England?"

"Not full-time, I suppose. I really don't know, but I doubt it. He'd have his life and I'd have mine." Robert shook his head to clear the idea that something like that would actually happen. "I have no idea how anything would work because it's almost laughable. I mean, if this thing were to come about, I don't have any delusions that it would be a love match or something. Arranged marriages have been done in the gentry for a thousand years."

Their conversation halted as their entrées arrived, lovely and beautifully garnished.

"Thank you," Daniel told the server and offered a smile. "This is obviously the place for the ladies who lunch."

"Definitely." Robert took his first bite of chicken salad and looked at Daniel, who did the same. "You know, this is okay…," he whispered.

"Yeah, but it definitely isn't the best I've ever had." Daniel shrugged, and they continued eating. "It's good, but not great."

"You pay for the location."

"Without a doubt." Daniel leaned over the table. "I'm glad we came because now I know I haven't been missing out."

Robert reached across the table. "Snootiness and snobbery are only ways of covering for inadequacy. It's like the man who drives the big fancy car. Chances are he's trying to make up for something." He snickered, and Daniel raised his pinkie. Robert lifted his napkin to his lips in order to stop from laughing out loud. "Exactly. So now you can continue eating the New York hot dogs gleefully, knowing you're getting exactly what you want."

They finished their meals, and Daniel grabbed the check when it came. He paid it while they had coffee, and then they left the hotel. "That was one illusion burst." He turned to look up at the hotel. "Where would you like to go next?" Daniel took Robert's arm and led him toward the sidewalk on Fifth. "We could walk if you like."

"Can we go to the Empire State Building?" Robert asked. "I've always heard about it and, of course, seen pictures on the telly…."

Daniel tensed. "Sure."

"What's wrong?" Robert asked. "And don't tell me 'nothing.' I can feel your tension."

"I hate heights."

"Oh," Robert said. "Then—"

"Oh, screw it. Let's go, and I'll deal with it. Just don't drag me to the railing or something, and I'll be fine." They continued down the sidewalk. Daniel released his arm, and they walked down one of the world's famous shopping streets, passing shop after shop.

"Have you ever thought about opening a store here? I know you sell online, but having a store would bring you visibility." Robert stopped in front of a smaller two-level clothing store. "Something like that."

"Actually, I have, and… we discounted it for the moment. The thing about selling online is that there's no overhead. I don't have to pay for real estate other than the office and warehouse. That storefront is god-awfully expensive, and I'd have to pay for that. I'd rather be able to sell a pair of custom boots for three hundred dollars than have to sell the same pair for four or five to pay for that space. Plus we figured we'd have to charge the same price if the customer came into the store or bought online, so in the end everyone, including the online customers, would end up paying for the storefront, and that isn't fair."

Robert gaped, open-mouthed. "I hate to say this, but you asked about me getting a businessperson to look at Ashton Park and come up with ideas. I think I found him."

"I have my own business to run."

"I'm not saying permanently. But you have a way of looking at things that is so very different from me, and that's what I need. Someone who will look at the place and give me the unvarnished truth."

Daniel turned from where he'd been looking in a shop window. "Are you asking me to be your Count of Hantford?"

Robert had no idea what to say to that. He hadn't, but Daniel was asking, and this… was too good to be true. Was Daniel teasing him? That had to be the only logical explanation. "Sure. Come to visit me in England and be my Count of Hantford." He could play along and have fun with this right along with Daniel. "Take a look at the place and tell me what you think."

"All right." Daniel grinned and began walking once again. "Let me see. From what you've told me, you have plenty of land. Have you raised sheep?"

"No, not personally, but it's perfect land for grazing."

"Then raise sheep for the wool, have it spun, and create a line of Ashton Park sweaters, mittens, and scarves of superior, top-quality wool, and limit production to the wool you produce. Nothing more. You control quality from beginning to end and make the brand something that becomes a status symbol that customers will pay amazing prices for."

"You're serious?" Robert said as the realization dawned on him.

"Of course. You have to fix the place up as well and open it for tours. From what little I know, you can probably work out a deal to defer inheritance taxes if it's open to the public so many days a year. That's what I understand a number of other families have done. Although it does make the family liable forever because if they stop, the taxes become payable. But it isn't like you want to live in the house alone for the rest of your life."

"No." They stopped at a corner, but Robert barely noticed. "I see myself as a caretaker. At first I thought about breaking the place up, maybe selling off some of the land. But it's been intact for ten generations, and I don't want to let that go. So somehow I have to figure out how to pass it on to the next generation, even though the family history isn't something I feel like I'm part of. My mother never talked about her family… ever. I think I met the former earl one time in my life, and I remember him and my mother fighting, and then my mother leaving with me in tow." Robert knew he'd said more than enough on this subject. They were out to have a good time, not talk about what was worrying him. "Are we getting close?"

The heat wafted off the streets and sidewalks. Robert needed a drink, and Daniel stopped to get something from a street vendor. With soda cans in hand, they continued on, the art deco building getting taller and taller as they walked toward it.

When they approached the building, they went to buy tickets, threw away their empty cans, and then stood in line to go up. Daniel appeared to grow more and more nervous as they entered in the elevator. The ride up was fast, and Daniel got greener the higher they went. He stepped off the elevator but stayed near the inside of the building. "You go—take pictures and have a good time. I'll be right here." He stood with his back to an interior wall, breathing deeply and slowly in and out.

"This was a bad idea." Robert led Daniel to the exit line.

"No. This is something everyone does when they're here, and you should see the city. That's why I brought you up here. So please go on, and I'll stay here. Have some fun."

Robert chuckled. "This is only fun because I'm doing this with you." He took Daniel by the hand and continued around the observation deck to where people were getting ready to leave.

"I'm okay now," Daniel told him and got out of the exit line. He pointed into the distance. "That's downtown, and you can see the Freedom Tower." They continued around. "Over there is the Chrysler Building. It's my favorite in the city. I love its style."

Robert wandered off after Daniel insisted once again, and he took some pictures of the city, looking out from all angles. Then he returned to Daniel and got him back to the ground.

"I'm sorry about all this," Daniel said.

"Hey, I'm the one who feels like a fool. You said you didn't like heights, so I should have picked something else to do." Robert led them away from Fifth Avenue and back toward his hotel. He knew where it was in relation to the Empire State. "I think we could both use a drink and maybe a chance to sit and relax."

"Oh God, yes." Daniel made a phone call. "The car service will have someone here as soon as they can. From now on we can drive rather than walk." They stood in the shade, and the car approached fifteen minutes later.

"Where to, sir?" the driver asked.

Daniel hesitated. He wanted to take Robert somewhere nice. Maybe it was time to break another self-imposed barrier. "King Cole Bar," Daniel instructed. "If we're going to have a drink, we may as well have one in style."

"You're going to spoil me." Robert shifted a little closer, and Daniel leaned on his shoulder.

"I think I'm still a little light-headed."

Robert put an arm around Daniel's shoulders as they rode through the city. It didn't matter where they were going. Robert was having a nice time, and when the driver turned, Daniel lifted his gaze and Robert kissed him.

"I've wanted to do that since the boat pond."

"Me too." Daniel kept the kiss gentle but intense, and Robert felt it to his toes. When the driver pulled to a stop, Daniel backed away and they got out. "We'll be about an hour. Can you pick us up?"

"Certainly." The driver tipped his hat, and Daniel closed the door and led the way inside.

"This is another icon in the city. The St. Regis is an amazing hotel, but it's the bar that everyone remembers." Daniel held the door and they easily got a table. "What's the drink special of the day?"

"We're famous for our Bloody Mary," the waitress said, so they both ordered one.

The interior was cool, and Robert looked over the richly decorated space with the famous painting behind the bar. The few people talking softly in hushed tones added a sense of reverence. "That's something."

"Yes, it is. I thought if you like, that we could go back to my apartment. I don't get to cook very often. When it's just me, I heat things up and work. But Joanne brought in groceries and took care of me, so I thought it might be nice."

"Are you sure?"

"Oh yes. I think I want to spend as much time as I can with you before you go back."

The server brought their drinks, and Robert sipped his, closing his eyes at the amazing mixture of flavors. "Damn," he groaned, opening his eyes to see Daniel leering at him, leaning closer.

"The sounds you make." The look in his eyes was pure heat and passion, leaving little doubt as to what Daniel was thinking about.

Robert's heart skipped a beat as it sped up. "It's a good drink."

"Yeah, but you know what they say. The sounds a man makes when enjoying a good drink are just the same as, only a quieter version of, the sounds he makes when...." Daniel's lips curled upward slightly, but he didn't finish his thought. Robert got the idea very clearly.

"Daniel...." Robert sipped his amazing drink and watched as Daniel did the same. Suddenly, watching Daniel's throat and wondering what he'd taste like was so much more interesting than the drink in front of him. Robert tipped his glass, not paying close enough attention, and nearly dribbled the deep orangey-red concoction down his shirt. He definitely needed to keep his focus where it belonged.

The tension between them built the longer they sat. Words didn't seem necessary as the air crackled around them with everything that went unsaid. Robert was starting to understand what it meant to be eye-fucked, because his breathing became shallower. He tried to concentrate on the painting behind the bar, his drink, the warmth of the room, but nothing touched the heat in Daniel's eyes. He finished his drink without spilling it, and Robert paid the bill this time. The car was waiting out front, and they got in. Daniel told the driver to take him home, and Robert wondered just how long it would take the heat between them to burst into flames.

CHAPTER 4

"MAKE YOURSELF comfortable," Daniel said once he'd unlocked his door and they'd stepped into air-conditioning. The temperature had continued to rise outside, so Daniel went right to the refrigerator and got two bottles of water. "This might help."

Robert took the bottle and opened it. "I'm not used to this kind of heat. It doesn't usually get this warm where I'm from."

"All the concrete doesn't help." Daniel sucked down the water and sat next to Robert. He hadn't been able to take his eyes off Robert for most of the afternoon, and this whole thing about finding someone to help him with the estate had Daniel intrigued. Robert had acted as though Daniel was kidding earlier about the whole count thing, but Daniel wasn't really sure how serious he was being. The idea of being called the Count of Hantford and having something to show the people he'd grown up with was a pretty powerful draw. Besides, he liked the idea of working to help Robert turn a worn-out estate profitable and bring it into the twenty-first century. Daniel had conquered the business world multiple times over, and this new challenge fascinated him.

"Thanks. The water is great." The bottle crinkled as Robert drank the last of it, and Daniel took the empty and tossed it into the recycling along with his.

"I'll start dinner in a while." He wasn't sure how to bring up the whole estate thing and figured he would have time to do that later. If he remembered, Robert was going to be here a few more days, so maybe they could have dinner and talk over a little more business. Today was about relaxing and having some fun. "I hope you got to see the things that were important to you."

"I did. When I got here, I was expecting to spend the day working and then maybe going out for dinner as the highlight of the day. I still have some things I have to do, but I figured I could get them done tomorrow."

"Can I get you anything else? Joanne got me some really nice Belgian and Irish beer." Daniel was up and to the refrigerator before Robert could answer. He just realized he probably should have had some way of entertaining Robert. If they just sat there, Daniel's thoughts would go to things he probably shouldn't be thinking about. For example, whenever Robert leaned a little closer to him, his scent filled the air and wrapped around Daniel like a pheromone bouquet with enough punch to drive him out of his head. He grabbed one of each bottle and showed them to Robert. "I like them both, so...."

Robert chose the Belgian, opened it, and sipped from the bottle. "Ever since I inherited, even the people I've known for years suddenly expect me to act differently. If I go out with them, they pick a fancier place." He closed his eyes. "Do you have any idea? It's been weeks since I could have a beer at the local pub without someone referring to me as 'my lord.' The barkeeper did it once, and I told him if he did it again, I'd never set foot in the place again."

"What did he do?" Daniel sat, then immediately got up to get some snacks and returned.

"You're like a little kid, aren't you? Unless you're moving or doing something, you aren't happy." Robert touched his shoulder, the warmth of his hand soothing him through his shirt.

"I'm sorry. I'm always used to having eight things to do and never enough time to get it all done. So I tend to go a mile a minute. But I don't think I'm needed that way any longer. Kick in the Pants is doing amazingly well, and so are the other ventures. I have good people I trust in positions of responsibility."

"Are you looking for something new and exciting?" Robert leaned back, and a look of relaxation settled over him.

"I think so." Daniel shifted and pulled his legs up under him. "I love what I do, but if I sit still for too long, I keep thinking that everything will pass me by. I have so many ideas that run around in my head, and sometimes I can't turn them off. All of my ideas start with the way I was raised. We didn't have much, so bargains and shopping wisely are important. No matter what kind of venture I undertake, I want the customer to get a value and to be purchasing things that they will be happy with and use for more than just a season. That's been true of men's fashion for years, but it should be true for women as well."

"It sounds like you found the recipe for success."

"I think so. But now I've done that and need something new. I'll find it, I'm sure. It's times like this when I usually come up with my best ideas." Daniel set his beer bottle on one of the coasters on the coffee table, grabbed a cracker, and put a little cheddar on it. "Is there anything else I can get you?"

Robert did the same with his bottle and turned so Daniel got a good look at his eyes. Doubt and worry slammed into Daniel like a sledge hammer. Robert had been talking all day about what had been on his mind, and Daniel thought it was just the normal "what am I going to do" kind of thing. But this was more than that.

"Jesus, Robert."

"Sorry. Sometimes it's hard to keep everything that's happened off my mind." What Daniel had seen for only a few seconds was gone, but it left a lasting impression.

"Come on. I think we need to do something else other than just sitting here. What kind of cook are you?" Daniel asked as he stood.

"Not much." Shrugging, Robert got up as well.

The whole idea that had been niggling around the edge of Daniel's mind came into focus, and he sighed. "Look. If you need someone to help with the estate, then I'm in a position to do something."

"Excuse me?" Robert said with a shake of his head, eyes showing nothing but disbelief.

"It would have to be a business relationship." Whatever had been going on between them would be a distraction, and Daniel didn't believe in distractions, not where money and everything he'd worked for came into play. "Think about what you need and how you might want to do this." Daniel went into the kitchen, not able to understand fully why he was saying this, but the idea had his mind going in multiple directions.

"Are you serious?" Robert asked, his mouth hanging open in what Daniel saw as shock.

"I think so, yes." He began getting the chicken he would add to the pesto pasta for dinner out of the refrigerator. It would be simple but good, and it was one of the dishes he knew he could make well.

"What brought this on? I know you were joking about it earlier...."

"I'm not sure. Part of it is the chance at a title. It would be awesome to walk into that reunion with it. But another piece of it is the challenge. I think I need that." He put water on to boil, and Robert joined him at the counter.

"So...."

"Like I said, it would be a business relationship. We seem to get along, so we aren't likely to be at each other's throats and all. We could help each other, I think. What I'm asking is that you put together how you expect this deal to work, and we can talk about it before you go back to England." The plan that had been forming in Daniel's mind solidified as they talked.

"Okay. If that's what you want." Robert perched himself on one of the stools, watching Daniel. "Can I ask you something? What about... well... what's been going on between us?"

Daniel sighed, adding pasta to the pot. "You need someone to help you get your estate back on its feet. I want to have the same title and position as the people I went to school with. I can go to my reunion and stand tall." God, he had dreaded going to that thing, and now he could look forward to it. "I know you and I started out with this whole matchmaker-slash-dating thing, but what I think you need is more of a business relationship." Daniel could deal with those kind of agreements so much better than he could a love life. The whole idea was sort of a relief. He could have what he wanted without all the head-cloudiness of romantic entanglements. Besides, this way, if things didn't work out—the way they hadn't with Theodore—there was no muss or heartbreak. They would simply dissolve their business partnership, divorce, and that would be the end of it. Daniel turned away and breathed a huge sigh of relief.

"A business relationship," Robert reiterated.

"Isn't that what you really had in mind when you contacted the matchmaker? After all, when most of the aristocracy married, they did so for advantage or to gain something they needed in return for a title. That's all we're doing now." Daniel seasoned the chicken as he cooked off the bite-sized pieces in a pan. Having something to do with his hands while he thought helped a lot.

"I suppose." Robert flashed him a gentle smile. "I'll think about it and put something together. I don't have an appointment, so if it's convenient for you, we can meet for dinner on Tuesday and hash out any remaining details before I fly home."

"Awesome." The tension that had been building between them still crackled. Daniel reduced the temperature on the chicken way down to finish cooking, checked the pasta, and turned off the water before draining it. "I can split my time between England and the US for a while. I'll have to work out visas and legal things like that. It's not as though I won't be able to be in touch on a regular basis. I think this can work out. If that's what you want, we can marry in the US and deal with the British legalities in time."

Daniel finished making dinner, dished up two plates, and brought them to the table. He also grabbed a bottle of white wine, popped the cork, and poured two glasses before sitting down. They began to eat, and this time the sexual tension between them could be cut with a knife. Daniel kept looking up at Robert, and each time his gaze sizzled back at him like a live wire. Daniel had asked for a business relationship but now wondered if that was even possible. Still, he'd been the one to propose the idea, and already his thoughts were turning much more carnal than any business relationship should ever be.

AFTER DINNER, Daniel took care of the dishes, and Robert waited until he was done before making sounds like it was time for him to go.

"Thank you for an amazing day."

"You're very welcome. It was pretty incredible for me too."

Daniel accompanied Robert to the door. He opened it, but Daniel pushed it closed once again. Robert returned Daniel's intense gaze, sending a flutter deep inside that Daniel felt to his very core. If he hadn't met this man, Daniel knew he would have missed something special. Daniel moved closer, but Robert placed his hand on Daniel's chest.

"You were the one who said our relationship should be a business one, and until I can think about what I can offer you, we have to keep it that way."

Daniel stepped back. He had said that, but Robert tended to make him forget himself. Maybe this idea of his wasn't such a good one after all. Mixing business with pleasure was a recipe for disaster. Daniel knew that well.

He took a deep breath. "You're right, of course." Still, Daniel couldn't help being disappointed and a little angry with himself that he'd opened his big mouth.

A SOUND rap on his door a few hours later stopped Daniel from tossing and turning. He checked the clock and groaned. There was only one person who'd bang on his door at six in the morning on a Sunday. He pushed back the covers and put on a robe, then padded to the living room and opened the door. Regina bounded inside as though she and Tigger were of the same species. He needed coffee, but giving her some would be like adding gasoline to an oil fire.

"Morning, Boo Boo." For some reason when she was six, she had decided they were going to play Yogi Bear and she'd deemed him Boo Boo. The game didn't last long, but the nickname did, at least with her, and Daniel cringed every time he heard it.

"If you're going to swear, you can go. I hate that name." Daniel closed the door with a little more force than was necessary.

"Good God, who fed you a poo sandwich?" She walked right around him to the kitchen.

"You're off the coffee. There's juice in the refrigerator. I don't need holes in my ceiling." Daniel scratched the back of his head. "What are you doing here? I thought you were in Paris or... somewhere." He tried to make his head work, but it felt as though he had a hangover even though he hadn't had much to drink.

"I was. But I needed to get back to New York for some meetings and to try to get some of the ready-to-wear collection in the department stores." She opened the refrigerator, poured two glasses of juice, and handed him one. "So what's new?" She sat at the table and stared at him.

"I'm going to kill Joanne," he muttered under his breath.

"No, you're not. That woman is a doll, and when I checked in to get on your schedule next week so we can talk over some ideas, she answered that you were off yesterday. On a date." She gulped her drink like it was a sailor's grog. "Dang, I needed that." She set the glass on the table. "You may as well tell me everything because you will in the end anyway."

"I have a stupid class reunion coming up, and Joanne thought I should bring a date." He really didn't want to talk about this, but Regina could be relentless and it was easier to give her what she wanted than to fight it. "She signed me up for a matchmaker,

71

and I had dinner with Robert Wednesday, and we spent the day together yesterday."

Regina stared at him, narrowing her eyes. "There's more to it than that. I can tell because you won't look at me. What did you do?" She pushed her glass away. "Let me guess. You spent the day talking about work, boots, and crap. God, sometimes you can be so boring."

"I can honestly say I wasn't boring." Daniel sat across from her. "I sort of entered into a possible new business venture." God, he saw just how crazy what he'd done actually was. "See, my date was with Robert and he's the Earl of Hantford. He just inherited the title and an estate. He's also a barrister working for people who need help and can't necessarily afford legal services. Robert is a really good guy."

"So what's wrong with this perfect earl? And what did you do?"

"I think I sort of agreed to marry him."

Regina threw her head back, her bark of laughter filling the kitchen. "No way in hell."

"He needs some help to fix up the estate, and if I marry him, then I can be the Count of Hantford. It would be a business deal, and we'd be partners in managing the estate. You know, getting it ready to open for tourists, putting the land to use, all that sort of thing."

Regina gaped at him. "Are you crazy and completely off your nut? You aren't some excess Vanderbilt heiress to marry off for a title and respectability, and this isn't a hundred years ago and all that shit."

"It's a business deal. Marriage would help protect the deal, and I get the title."

"Marriage is not some kind of business deal." She glared at him hard, her eyes boring into him as though they had cartoon drills. "There's more to this than just some business deal that will also make you a count. Though wouldn't you technically be the countess?" She put her hand over her mouth, laughter showing in her eyes.

"I know it sounds crazy. But like I said, it would be a business deal. And we can reevaluate the situation in two years if we want to change it."

Her laughter died to chuckles. "This is crazy, Boo. You're seriously going to marry some guy you barely know so you can be Count... whatever."

"There's more to it than that. Robert needs help, and this could be another challenge. It would definitely be something different."

"I know you're getting antsy for another project. But marrying someone—"

"It isn't as though I'm marrying him tomorrow or anything. We agreed to talk things over and work through a business plan."

Regina rolled her eyes. "No wonder you never found someone. You think finding a husband is a business deal. You like this guy, don't you?" She grinned. "You're hiding behind some façade of business, but you really like him. I know it. That's why you're doing this crap. You like him but you're afraid. Not everyone is going to leave you, ya know."

"That isn't it." His rebuttal seemed weak.

"Sure it is. You like him." Regina stood and went back to the refrigerator. "God, don't you ever cook? Everything is premade." She closed the door. "Get dressed. You're taking me out for breakfast." She plopped herself back into the chair. "I know you well enough to know that when you've set your mind to something, you'll follow through and somehow make a success out of it. But promise me a few things. That you'll treat the business part of this deal carefully—"

He nodded his agreement.

"—and that if you really like this guy, you'll do something about it."

Daniel sighed. "Fine. I like him. Robert is a very interesting man, and—"

"Is he sex on a stick?" Regina asked, cutting to the chase as usual.

"He's handsome, and…." Damn, he couldn't hold in his smile. "Yes. Robert is sexy. And fine, I like him—I really do." He was glad he was at a table so his sister couldn't see the reaction he was having just thinking about him.

"You do what you want. But I want to meet him before you do anything permanent. You're my brother, and you marrying anyone is more than business. So I get to meet him."

"Of course you'll meet him—eventually. I'm seeing him on Tuesday before he flies back Wednesday. And I'll plan a trip over there to spend more time with him and to see the estate. There are a lot of things that need to be worked out."

"I know you'll take care of business, but I want you to make sure you're taking care of yourself. If you marry someone you aren't in love with…." She shook her head. "Just be careful, okay?"

"Of course I will."

"Good. Now go get dressed so you can feed me something more than juice." She turned away, and Daniel hurried to his bedroom before Regina could see the actual evidence of just what thinking about Robert did to him. That alone was almost enough to make things go south.

CHAPTER 5

ROBERT WAS nervous beyond belief. He'd left New York two weeks earlier, and he and Daniel had talked over what had to be the craziest deal between two people in the history of modern society. Daniel had actually agreed to come to Ashton Park to see the estate, and the plan was that if everything worked out, they'd get married. It would have to be in the US because of strange reciprocation laws, but that was fine. The thing was, even though they'd approached this like a business deal, the part of Robert that came alive when he slept didn't seem to be getting the message at all. His dreams for two weeks had been vivid and as unbusinesslike as possible.

"Robert, are you sure about this?" his mother asked from the passenger seat as they approached Heathrow. His mother had been nice enough to get up extra early to keep him company on the long ride.

"I'm not sure about anything. But Daniel is willing to help finance the restoration of Ashton Park, provided that I'm willing to marry him. He'd get a title and he'd be part owner of the estate. However, he did accept that if we could get the estate profitable again, he'd split the profits with me, and as long as his investment was paid back eventually, the house and land would pass to my heirs, which is what was important."

"I'm not worried about the land and house, but you." His mother patted his leg gently. "You've been jittery and quick to snap ever since you got back from the States, and I'm worried that this may be more than you bargained for."

"It's fine, Mum. Daniel is a nice man, and according to everything I can find out about him, he'll do what he says he'll do. He's a man of his word."

"Then what's the problem?" She sat back as Robert continued his drive into London. "It isn't like you'll be married forever."

"I know. We'll work together—and just happen to be married—for a few years, and then we'll get Ashton Park back to where it should be and bringing in revenue. Then we can go our separate ways. It's a business relationship and nothing more. At least that's what Daniel said he wanted."

"And you don't…," she said. "You really like Daniel. I can tell. Every time you've mentioned him for the last two weeks, you get flustered and turned around." She turned away to look out the window as they approached the outskirts of the city. "I think it's cute."

"Mum. I thought he liked me when we were in New York, but then I told him about the estate and what I wanted. He decided that he'd help me, but just as a business arrangement. It's like he's only interested in the title and what he'll get out of the deal. I thought he liked me, but suddenly it was all business. We talked deals and agreements and—"

"Sweetheart. He's giving you what you wanted."

"I know."

"You knew him for a few days and he's going to help you. So take what you can get for now and see what else happens. If he liked you before he found out about the earldom, then he'll like you down the road."

"I think you're being naive."

She turned to him with a look that would freeze boiling water in two seconds. "Just see what he has to say. After all, this Daniel has come all this way to see you."

"He's coming to see Ashton Park," Robert corrected.

"You don't know that. You spent time with him in New York." Her expression softened. "Did he kiss you?"

Robert continued driving and didn't answer.

"Did he?"

"Yes."

"And how was it? Because a man can lie about many things, but not about that." She grinned. "When I met your father, he didn't think he was good enough and pushed me away because he didn't want me to have to give up my life to be with him. He was going to go to America, and I told him I wanted him to kiss me once before he left. I knew in that moment that he loved me."

"Yes. He kissed me, and yes, it was…." God, how did he describe the kiss to his mother?

"Then things will work out. You just have to have a little faith. Besides, who in their right mind could resist you?" She reached over to pinch his cheek.

"You do know that I'm no longer twelve." Traffic got heavier by the minute, and Robert followed the signs to Heathrow. "Can you check that his flight is on time? The page is already loaded."

She checked his phone. "Yes. It lands in fifteen minutes. You know it hasn't changed since the last time you checked." She set the phone down, and Robert drove the rest of the way.

He parked in the most convenient lot, and they walked inside to where Daniel would exit customs. "There he is," Robert said to his mother as Daniel stepped through the doorway.

"Honey…. He can butter my toast any time."

"Mum!"

"Well, he can." She was already moving forward. "Daniel Fabian, I'm Isabelle Morton, Robert's mother, and it's so nice to meet you."

Daniel took her hand and shook it gracefully. "I've been looking forward to meeting you since Robert and I set up this trip. Robert, you didn't tell me your mother was so beautiful." He smiled at her, and it was obvious Robert's mother was eating it up. Daniel could be very charming. That was probably part of his business success.

"Please. I stopped being beautiful some time ago," she scolded, though Robert knew she was taken by the compliment.

"Do you have all your bags?" Robert asked. When Daniel nodded, Robert led the way out of the airport. In New York, the time they'd spent together had been so easy and fun, but now everything seemed important. "We're parked right over there."

"Awesome."

"Before we leave, I need to use the ladies' room." His mother excused herself, and just like that, Robert was alone with Daniel.

"How was your flight?"

"Long but smooth. Thank you for picking me up. I could have arranged for a car to take me out."

"No. I wanted to come." Robert glanced at the arrivals board blankly. "I really hope you like Ashton Park."

"I got the pictures you sent, and I'm looking forward to seeing it. I have some ideas that we can talk over. I made a list of them on the plane. Of course, they may all change once I see the building, but we can discount any that we don't think will work. And I'm hoping there will be new ones that come to mind."

"I don't want to change the integrity of the building, and anything we do shouldn't cause any harm."

"Of course not. This is a building that has been here for hundreds of years and it needs to be around for hundreds more. That was one of the goals you told me, and I listened. Besides, the value of the property is in its history and all that represents." Daniel paused. "And I know that's what's important to you personally. If continuity wasn't a priority, you wouldn't be doing this." For a few seconds, Daniel caught his gaze with some of the intensity he'd shown that day in New York when they'd been in the boat on the lake. Daniel took his hand. "I promise. We are most definitely on the same page with this."

Robert nodded, unable to speak as he sank a little into Daniel's expressive eyes. God, this whole deal was going to be more difficult than he imagined. Standing next to Daniel, his scent wafted over to him, tickling his nose. "I'm glad." He saw his mother returning across the concourse and was grateful for the chaperone. "Right out this way." Robert took one of Daniel's bags, and Daniel offered his mother an arm as they headed toward the exit.

"Robert told me that you grew up at Ashton Park." Daniel set his bag aside and held the door before grabbing the luggage handle again.

"I did. It was a glorious place then. But times were different. I see now that we were probably enjoying the last hurrah before everything changed forever."

"That could be true, but Robert and I are going to do our best to bring the old girl back where she should be." Daniel sounded so positive.

"Do you think it's possible?"

The hope in his mother's voice was almost too much for Robert. He'd been keeping the extent of the repairs required from her. There was no need for him to tell her all the details. She still thought of Ashton Park as someplace where she'd been happy as a child. Robert didn't want to damage those memories.

"Of course. I have a feeling that if you put the two of us together, Robert and I can accomplish just about anything."

"My Robert is quite a man," his mother said.

"Yes, he is," Daniel agreed, meeting Robert's gaze.

He kept getting so many mixed signals from Daniel that it was hard for him to understand what was happening. Maybe it was just his freer American ways, and the flirting was just a part of who he was. "Mother, I'm right here."

"Of course you are, dear." She patted Daniel's arm and then released it as Robert popped open the boot.

"Is it okay if I work a little while we ride? I need to catch up on what happened while I was in the air." Daniel put his larger bag inside, then took his smaller bag from Robert.

"Of course." Robert closed the boot, and they got in.

"It used to be that the earl never rode in the front seat of the car," Robert's mother commented.

"Robert isn't the same kind of earl." Daniel pulled out his phone, staring at it. "That's the reason I'm helping him. Robert is down-to-earth and willing to do what needs to be done. If he was all about position, maintaining some style of living above what he could afford, I wouldn't be here."

"I see," his mother said.

"I mean it." Daniel glanced at Robert's mother. "Robert is going to be a great earl because he's less interested in the trappings of the title and more inclined to try to make the earldom a successful business that can carry on into the future. As we say, he has a good head on his shoulders. Maybe if so many past earls hadn't been so intent on sitting in the backseat and did more for themselves, then the earldom wouldn't be in the state it is now."

Daniel returned his attention to his phone, and Robert noticed his mother sat in silence.

DANIEL WORKED much of the way in the car, and Robert wasn't sure if he was upset about it or not. Daniel seemed so intent on what he was doing, only glancing to look out the window every now and then before returning his attention to his phone or tablet. He seemed to have multiples of each and moved back and forth between them for hours.

"There," he said quietly, and Robert glanced in the mirror to see Daniel had set everything aside. "Hopefully everyone has what they need from me today."

"I understand you sell boots," Robert's mother said to Daniel.

"Yes, I brought Robert a pair. We scanned his feet when he was in New York, but delivery was going to take too long, so I brought them with me." Daniel touched his shoulder. "I hope you like them."

"I'm sure I will." Robert smiled without looking away from the road. Daniel had remembered that he'd wanted a pair. Of course, he shouldn't read too much into it. Daniel was probably just being nice.

"You only brought a few bags," Robert's mother said. "Are you sure you're going to have enough of what you need?"

"I wasn't sure how to pack, so instead of bringing everything, I got what I thought I'd need and figured I could buy anything else. There was no need to cart half my place over here at this point." Daniel leaned forward, looking out between the seats. "It's very pretty here. Are we going to your home or right to Ashton Park?"

"I thought we'd go home first. That way you can clean up if you like and get some rest. Then we'll go to Ashton Park tomorrow, and we can spend the day reviewing what's there and working through ideas."

"Sounds good." Daniel turned to the side and covered his mouth. "Sorry. I didn't sleep very well on the plane, and it's still the small hours of the morning back home."

His mother patted Daniel's arm. "It happens to all of us. The last time I was in the States, it took days for me to recover."

"I didn't know you'd gone to the US on holiday," Robert said.

"Don't you remember? Maybe not. We took you to Florida to Disney World when you were a boy. Your dad saved for almost a year so we could make the trip."

"Yeah, I guess I do. I just hadn't thought about it that way." Robert settled back in the seat, trying to let go of the tension that seemed to be intensifying every time a hint of Daniel's breath caressed up his neck. Holy hell, this whole business-relationship thing was going to be the death of him. Hell, Robert had never been so grateful for loose trousers in his life, though if Daniel didn't sit back soon, Robert was going to put on a display of trouser-tent action that he certainly didn't want his mother to see.

The turnoff was just ahead, thank God, and Daniel sat back as Robert made the turn and continued through.

While his mother's cottage was quaint and had old-world charm, his small house was modern but affordable. He helped Daniel in with his luggage while his mother went right to the kitchen.

"You're going to be hungry. It isn't as though they feed you anything decent on the plane."

"Come on. I'll show you to your room." Robert hefted Daniel's large bag and went up the stairs to the guest room. The bedrooms were small in the house, including his, but he liked to think it was welcoming.

"This is nice, and the breeze...." Daniel went right over to the window, opened it, and peered outside.

"I hope you'll be comfortable." Knowing what to say was harder than he expected.

"I'm sure I will be." Daniel turned away from the window, set his smaller bag on the floor, and unzipped it. He pulled out two cloth bags and set them in Robert's hands.

"These are amazing," Robert said softly when he pulled the boots out of their bags. "I didn't...." They had to be some of the most expensive boots Daniel's company made. The buttery-soft leather practically flowed under Robert's hands.

"You're the earl, and I wanted to bring you something special."

For some strange reason, Robert felt like the boots were a sort of engagement gift.

"I meant what I said in the car. You are a particularly amazing man with both feet on the ground, so I thought those feet deserved to be in something equally special."

"Thank you." Robert blinked as he tried once again to get his mind around what was going on between them. He liked that things were heating up and would love nothing more than to get a good peek at exactly what Daniel looked like under his formfitting jeans and intense white shirt that appeared as if it had just been pressed as opposed to going through a transatlantic flight. That so wasn't fair. After making one of those flights himself, Robert always looked like an unmade bed when he landed. "Well, I'll leave you to it, then. Mum will have food on shortly." He turned to leave but Daniel placed his hand on his shoulder. Robert stilled and closed his eyes, not sure what was going on, figuring he'd wait to see what Daniel did. But his hand slipped away again.

He left the guest room, and put the boots in his room before joining his mother in the kitchen.

"You don't cook much and yet your kitchen has better things than mine."

"That's because mine are new and yours have been used for decades." He walked to where she was working and kissed her on the cheek.

"What's got you so flustered?" she asked in a whisper.

"He confuses me."

She laughed. "Men—gay or not, you're all alike."

"How so?" Robert wasn't sure if he should be offended for his entire gender or not.

"Look. Men don't always say what they mean, no matter how much you all like to think you're straight shooters. So Daniel said he wanted this relationship to be a business one, and maybe it will be. Keep the business part business and make any personal part of your relationship just that. It's not that hard—people do it all the time."

"So what should I do?" Robert couldn't believe he was asking for relationship advice from his mother.

"Whatever you want to. This isn't something with a lot of rules. It's your life."

He sighed. "I always thought I'd be in love with someone before I married him. He and I have talked marriage so that I can fix up the estate and he can get a title, but so far there hasn't been one word about kindness or passion. Nothing. You gave up a lot because you loved Dad."

"Yes, I did, and if I had it to do over, I wouldn't change a thing. We had a wonderful life, and I want that same thing for you."

"So you're saying I should call this whole thing off?"

"He's here. You're here. See what happens. I know this whole idea sounded crazy to begin with, and it's even more unusual now that Daniel has agreed at least in some way to be a part of it." She took the pan with the eggs off the heat and set it aside. "I like him. I think he has spunk and isn't afraid to speak his mind. I also saw the way he looked at you sometimes, and I saw how you kept looking in the rearview mirror. There's something between you. Don't let this 'business' thing get in your way. Don't forget you're a Hantford, and that means that we're pretty good at getting what we want. Even if some of us can be real bastards about trying to bring it about, like your uncle."

"So I should stop worrying?" Robert asked and heard footsteps from behind him. He turned around and saw Daniel filling the doorway of the kitchen. He'd changed into lightweight pants and a T-shirt that hugged his upper arms.

"If you don't want to go for him, I'd sure like a shot," his mother whispered, and Robert ignored her. In those clothes, Daniel was a tall drink of water, to use one of the Yankee expressions he'd heard, and it certainly fit Daniel, especially with the slight western cut to the shirt.

"Please, sit down." Robert found his voice and helped bring the food to the table before pouring juice. Once his mother dished up, they settled down to eat.

"Robert told me that you grew up in Texas."

"Yes, ma'am." Daniel's accent came out heavily, and Robert realized he could listen to him all day. The lilt, the flow of his speech, was sexy, and when Daniel brushed the hair off his forehead as though he were habitually adjusting his hat, he wondered what Daniel would look like in one. "It was just my mom and sister for most of my life, and my mom, she had to do it all."

"I bet she's something," his mother said, and Robert tried to signal her.

"She's gone. Basically there's just my sister and me. Right now she's back in New York after a quick trip to Milan. We sort of passed by each other over the Atlantic on this trip. She's promised me that she'll be there when I get home." Daniel took a bite of his eggs and made yummy sounds. "You're a very good cook, ma'am."

"Please call me Isabelle, and thank you."

"Mum learned how to cook after she married my dad."

Isabelle chuckled. "My Peter, rest his soul, had to teach me how to cook once we were living on our own. It was one of the things he and I did together for a long time. After Peter taught me, I always loved cooking because it was something we shared." She turned away, and Robert touched her shoulder. His mother was not an overly emotional person, so to see her act like this, in front of someone she'd just met, was pretty.... Well, Robert didn't have words, and he was supposed to be good with the damn things. He just couldn't believe it.

"My mom made sure both Regina and I knew how to cook. She always said that she wanted us to be able to feed ourselves in case she wasn't there to do it."

"Okay." Robert had to step in. "This is getting too maudlin for color telly right now. Mum, Daniel just got here. Let's let him settle in and get some rest before we start regaling him with stories. Especially ones that involve me in nappies." He knew those were coming next. He could feel it.

They finished breakfast without making anyone cry or blush, and Daniel went up to his room to rest.

"He's something else. I like him."

"So do I, Mum."

"Then don't worry so much. If it's meant to be, then it will happen, and nothing he says about business deals—or anything else—will stand in the way. You're two gay blokes who will be living and working side by side for part of the time at least. Pure horniness is bound to take over."

"Mum!"

"Am I wrong?" she pressed.

"Probably not. But when did you start talking like that?"

"Since my son became an earl and I realized I've been sitting here in my cottage puttering around since your father died. If you're going to be an earl, then I get to be your interesting, wild, say-anything mother."

"Just be yourself. This person you're trying to be is a little frightening."

"Robert. I've been dull and quiet for too long. I want my life to be more interesting, and the only way that is going to happen is if I'm more interesting."

He didn't understand where she was coming from exactly. Robert had always thought she had been happy. But maybe she wanted more than her current lot in life, the way most people did. "What are your plans for the rest of the day?"

His mum wiped her hands on a dishcloth and hung it up. "I cooked, so I'm leaving you with the washing up, and I'll walk home. I think I'm going to spend my afternoon in my garden."

He kissed her good-bye, and then Robert logged into his computer to get some work of his own done.

THE REST of the day was uneventful. Daniel was more jet-lagged than he thought, so Robert was quiet and let him rest. The following morning, Robert packed a hamper for lunch, along with water, juice, and some sodas and went in to check on Daniel.

He was sound asleep when Robert quietly pushed the door open. The room was warm, and Daniel had squirmed or twisted the covers off him and lay on the bed, facedown, naked as the day he was born. Robert's British sensibilities told him to back away and forget what he was looking at, but that backside on glorious display was too good to turn away from. Robert felt like a voyeur, but Daniel was an incredible man. He let his gaze sweep down Daniel's broad shoulders and the small of his back, to the swell of an arse that would do any sculptor proud. Robert had been taught from an early age that God had made man in his image, and he had just found living proof.

He back out, closed the door, and knocked softly. "Daniel?"

Heavy footsteps sounded and the door cracked open. "Yeah."

"Are you ready to go?" Of course Robert knew he wasn't, but what else could he do?

"What time is it?" Daniel rubbed his eyes.

"Half past eight."

"Crap. Give me a few minutes and I'll be out." He closed the door, and Robert went back to the kitchen. There had been times when he'd wished he could unsee things. This morning's view was something he'd probably recall for the rest of his life.

When Daniel joined him, his face was unshaved and his hair still mussed, but Robert really didn't care. It made Daniel look more rugged, and that was one hell of a turn-on.

"I have some coffee for you."

"Oh God. I love you for that." Daniel took the cup and groaned as he sipped. Within a few minutes, Daniel had finished his cup and his eyes seemed less glazed. "I'm ready to go whenever you are."

Robert grabbed the hamper and led the way out to the car. "I talked to the tax people last week," Robert told Daniel while he drove toward the estate. "They said there was precedent for deferring the taxes on Ashton Park as long as we plan to open the estate to the public for sixty days a year at minimum. I've looked into selling the property in London and can get a high price for it just because of the location. I was quoted over a million pounds by an agent, and they said that as long as I route the funds generated directly to Ashton Park, then they would defer those taxes as well."

"Do you want to sell the London house?"

"No. It's a grand old thing with woodwork and moldings that would be impossible to replicate. So I'm thinking of selling my home to raise some of the funds and then... I don't know."

"That's okay." Daniel's voice sounded so soothing. "We'll work everything out one step at a time."

"What do you suggest?"

"We assess the condition of Ashton Park and determine what it really needs. I did some research and looked up the firms that did restoration work on other estates, and I called a few of them to check their availability. They were all chomping at the bit to work with you. The National Trust has resources that can help as well."

"So what do I do?"

"Call this man. He's the one at the National Trust who I spoke with. He said he'd be more than willing to come out. He's worked on a number of other properties and said he was more than qualified to help with an assessment."

"You don't let grass grow under your feet, do you?" Robert said.

"Nope. But there are some things I know. First, any work on the basic structure needs to be done to secure the building from the elements. Then the work inside can begin. Plumbing and electrics have to be done so they don't disturb the integrity of the walls. We'll assess what we have and go from there."

"How do you know so much?"

"In high school I worked construction. I'm not an electrician or a plumber, but I worked with them so I know the general order of things."

"That's good." Robert continued driving, trying to keep up with everything Daniel was throwing at him. "We're getting close." He pulled off the main road and out into the country. The towers peeked above the trees, and then Robert pulled up to the gate. Gene hurried across the yard to open the gate, let them in, and closed it after they passed through. Robert stopped, and Gene approached his window.

"We were looking for you, your lordship," Gene said, and Robert lowered his gaze. "I mean… Robert."

"Thank you."

"I hope it's okay. But you said that the estate could afford some help for me, so I brought in two of my brothers. Mason is amazing with growing things, and Dicken can fix just about anything. He's up on the roof now and says that he found the real problem behind our leak and can fix it for us."

"That's good news. Thank you." Robert leaned back. "Gene, I want you to meet Daniel Fabian. He's my fiancé. Why don't you meet us up at the house so we can go over what we think needs doing?" When Gene nodded, showing little surprise at his announcement, and stepped back, Robert pulled down the drive and up to the front entrance. "I hope it's okay if I refer to you that way." They hadn't talked it over and the word had just come out.

"Of course. It's what we are, I guess." Daniel flashed him a smile and then turned to look out the window once again. "Wow. It's stunning." Daniel opened the door and got out, standing next to the car, looking up. "Do you know the history?"

"Not really." Robert got out and joined him, trying to get the brain-clouding effect of Daniel's smile out of his head.

"Then we need to piece it together. It's a stunning place, and if we decide to fix it up and open it to the public, we have to have some sort of hook to get them in. Who were guests here? Did something of world importance happen here? If there's something that will capture people's imagination, then it becomes much easier to market." Daniel's gaze didn't shift from the stone façade.

"Yes."

"The stonework seems in remarkable shape. It's stained by water and wear, but looks okay to me. But the gutters are failing and that's putting rainwater near the building, which can affect the foundation. So channeling water away from the structure is a priority."

"Robert," Gene said as he approached, and Robert shook hands with him. "These are my brothers, Mason and Dicken."

Robert shook both their hands. It was clear they were brothers, evidenced by the same slim build, wild dark hair, and eyes nearly as black as coal. "It's good to meet both of you. This is my fiancé, Daniel Fabian." He stepped back so Daniel could shake hands.

"Do you know buildings like this?" Gene asked Daniel.

"Oh, no. I worked in construction so I know some of the basics, but this is the first time I've ever seen anything like this."

"Gene and I have been working on the roof," Dicken explained.

"Dicken found the real weak spot, and we removed the tiles and replaced the wood underneath before putting them back. The last time it rained, we came here and checked inside. It's watertight for now."

"Thank you." Daniel knew that was definitely good news.

Gene unlocked the door for them, and they stepped inside. The sun shone into the entrance hall, furniture still enshrouded in dustcovers. "The power and water have been shut off to most of the house for safety reasons. There are a few rooms with power. Your uncle had the rooms he used some time ago rewired, and that's where there are electrics. We don't turn on the rest of the house just in case," Gene explained.

"Okay. We knew about the power upgrades, and plumbing can be checked and upgraded when necessary," Daniel said as he looked through the hall. "My God. Do you know what's under the covers?"

"No," Robert answered along with Gene.

"How is the foundation?"

"Solid," Gene answered. "The house sits on a very slight rise, but it is enough to keep water away."

"It looks like you've gotten lucky in a few ways. If the foundation was going, that would be a major blow and cost to repair. The roof, wiring, and plumbing are plenty, and, of course, there will be other hidden issues that we'll find as soon as we start work on something else." Daniel turned to Gene. "What else do you know that will need to be done? I suppose the entire below-stairs servant area will need to be looked at."

"Yes, sir." Gene shifted slightly on his feet.

"Please call me Daniel."

"I'm also going to suggest that as part of the work, we might consider a climate-control system, and I bet new heating is a must.

We should also bring in some art experts to assess what we have here. There are paintings and goodness knows what else in the house."

Robert's head was beginning to spin. "I thought of that. We should also visit the climate-controlled storage unit where my uncle transferred the books and some other items."

"Have you been there?" Daniel asked.

"Yes. But everything is packed away in wooden crates and boxes, and I didn't want to disturb anything until we were ready."

"Good point." Daniel turned to Gene. "You know this building better than anyone, so why don't you take us on a tour?"

They followed Gene, Mason, and Dicken as they showed them through the manor, pointing out areas that they thought would need work. Daniel had his tablet and made notes. After two hours of going through everything room by room, Robert was thirsty, hungry, and a little worn out. He was also incredibly discouraged as the list got longer and the amount of money it was going to take to do all these repairs continued to mount. When they returned to the main hall, Gene handed him a key and then followed his brothers outside, closing the door.

"That was eye-opening," Daniel said when he turned to Robert. "I knew this was going to be a big job, but I don't think I understood the scope of it."

"Is it too much? I know we talked about the broad outlines of our dealings, but if it's too much, just walk away and I'll figure out what I'm going to do."

Daniel took a step closer. "I think this is a real challenge. Do you have any idea how this looks to a kid from Texas? Everything there was new and looked like it just sprouted out of the ground yesterday, and this seems like it's been part of the very earth forever. This place has a history, and to be part of that...."

"Daniel, is that all you really want?" The confusing signals were getting to him.

Before he could answer, the light from outside the shuttered windows dimmed. Daniel opened one of them near the door and peered out. "We might be in for some rain. At least we can verify that the roof is truly fixed for now."

Thunder rumbled in the distance, and it took Robert a second to recognize it. They got rain quite frequently, but thunder was a bit of a rarity. His stomach tensed and fluttered unpleasantly.

"Why don't I get the basket out of the trunk and we can have lunch while it rains?"

Robert nodded, though the last thing he wanted at that very moment was food.

Daniel opened the outside door as thunder rumbled again, this time a little closer. Robert grabbed his keys from his pocket and opened the boot with the fob. Daniel returned with the hamper, running inside as the wind picked up, swirling inside the house, fluttering the dustcovers that hung over everything. Robert closed the door and leaned against it briefly.

"We may as well go into the sitting room. There was furniture in there, and we can see the kind of shape it's in." Daniel led the way, and Robert followed, listening and trying like hell not to jump at the next clap of thunder.

Daniel gently set the hamper next to a covered sofa and carefully rolled up the cover. Even in the dim light, the tapestry fabric shone a little, as though happy to see the light of day once again.

"This is the ladies' sitting room," Robert explained as Daniel removed the cover on a nearby table. The inlay was stunning.

Daniel looked around. "How about we sit on the floor? I think it'll be safer."

He spread out the dustcover like a blanket, and Robert sat down. Daniel opened a few of the shutters to let a little more light in and then joined him. Robert wasn't too sure how happy he was when lightning flashed once again, followed almost immediately by the thunder. He was about ready to jump out of his skin.

"What is it?"

"I hate storms. I know it is silly, but you have the height thing and I have the thunder-and-lightning thing." He wasn't supposed to admit it to anyone. "I'll be all right."

"Hey." Daniel scooted around to sit next to him, and then Robert was engulfed in a pair of warm, strong arms, holding him tight. It was as though the storm couldn't touch him, at least at that moment.

"I'll be all right. You don't have to do this."

Daniel didn't move away. "You're my fiancé, remember? That's what you called me twice today."

"I know you're here and all, and I know what we talked about, but we don't have to do this. The house needs a lot of work, but getting married…. Is a title really all that important?"

Daniel leaned a little closer. "I like being thought of as your fiancé." He tugged Robert nearer, and the thunder shook the building. Robert closed his eyes, clinging to Daniel, who stroked his back and tried to soothe away the irrationality of fear. "Just relax. This house has weathered storm after storm for centuries now. It will get through this one." Daniel stroked his cheek, and when Robert lifted his face away from his shoulder, Daniel kissed him. This was no gentle, reassuring kiss, but filled with as much energy as the storm outside. Robert held on tight, reciprocating as Daniel pressed him back onto the floor.

Robert broke the kiss and stilled. "I thought we were going to keep things businesslike between us," he panted, light-headed. He barely registered the next roll of thunder as it shook the manor.

"I know what I said, and I was so stupid. I've looked forward to this trip for weeks, and I never look forward to a business meeting. I thought it would be the best thing in case it didn't work out. This whole idea is a little crazy, but after seeing you and this place… I could be part of something lasting." Daniel's gaze bored into him. "We could be part of something lasting," he corrected, and Robert wasn't sure if he was referring to the manor house or to them.

Robert closed the distance between them, devouring Daniel's lips and cutting off further conversation. God, he'd dreamed of this for weeks. He clung to Daniel as a storm as intense as the one outside raged in Robert, threatening to break free. He wanted to feel Daniel against him. The glimpse he'd gotten that morning had only whetted his appetite. Robert let go of his British reservation and yanked Daniel's shirt out of his pants and tugged it off.

Daniel leaned back and did the same to him. They wrestled on the floor, each pawing to get the other's clothes removed. Robert toed his shoes off, and they slid along the wooden floor, followed by Daniel's. Somehow Robert managed to kick off his pants with a little too much enthusiasm and they ended up over the back of a dust-covered chair, but Robert couldn't have cared less.

"Jesus," Daniel whispered as he sat back, running his hands down Robert's belly.

"I know. I never did get any sun at all, and…." Robert had always hated that he was as pale as a ghost.

Daniel leaned forward, kissed the center of his chest, and then downward, licking a trail and sending Robert on one hell of a joyride. "You're stunning."

"No, I'm not."

Daniel's gaze intensified. "Yes, you are, Earl Robert. God, that's really sexy."

Robert had no idea why, but when Daniel ground his cotton-clad erection against his, he really didn't care anymore. Robert pressed his hands to Daniel's chest, stroking slowly, the banked power and strength flowing to him. Daniel was so strong and sure of himself. Most of the time Robert liked to think of himself as being the same, and in the courts, he was. But the last couple of months had thrown him way out of his comfort zone and he hadn't been sure where to turn. Daniel's strength helped him feel safe, like he had a direction, and that a plan was possible to move forward.

"I never thought I could catch the eye of someone like you."

"Me?" Daniel brushed the edges of Robert's upper lip with his tongue. "You're the one who's too hot for words. You act reserved, but your eyes have this quiet intensity and you have a rod of steel in your back. No matter what you think is going to happen or how much you doubt yourself, you're going to be an amazing earl, and the people in this area are going to respect and trust you for who you are."

"How do you know?" Robert asked breathily.

"I can feel it." Daniel placed his hand over Robert's heart, held it there, and leaned closer to suck on his upper lip. Daniel kept his hand on his chest, and Robert wondered if Daniel could feel his heart hammering beneath it.

When Daniel lifted his hand away, he brought his fingers to Robert's mouth and traced it. Robert sucked Daniel's digits between his lips, running his tongue over them, moaning as Daniel's flavor burst on his tongue. Daniel stroked down Robert's belly to the elastic of his underwear. He didn't stop, sliding his fingers underneath. Robert gasped and groaned deep in his throat, closing his eyes, and Daniel gripped his cock in a firm grasp.

"That's it."

"What?" Robert thought his eyes were going to cross on their own.

"That sound. You made it over good food in New York, and I wondered how it would sound when you were about to completely lose yourself." Daniel squeezed and stroked, drawing Robert out of his underwear. "It's the most beautiful thing I have ever heard in my life." Daniel released him, to Robert's dismay, but then stripped him naked. Robert stared up at him as Daniel stripped off the last of his own clothes. Then Daniel tossed them aside, knelt, and covered him, chest to chest, their legs entwining, and pummeled his lips as he moved along with him.

"I'm…. I don't—"

"What is it?"

"It's been a long time," Robert managed breathily.

He gasped for air as Daniel thrust his hips slowly, his cock sliding along Robert's, stealing his breath that such a simple pleasure could mean so very much. Daniel held him tight. Lightning lit the sitting room and thunder cracked, sinking into Robert's soul. He should have been scared for his life. He usually was in storms like this, but Daniel was here with him, holding him, touching his soul, and nothing else mattered.

Robert ran his hands down Daniel's back to grab his firm, smooth arse, the one he'd stared at that morning. He held on for dear life, grinding up against Daniel, letting ecstasy take over. "You feel so good." Robert poured all he had into sharing what he felt at that moment. The storm seemed to be building, pushing him on rather than driving his fear. Robert arched his back, the floor hard under him. He felt them shift more and more as the dustcover slid on the wood, Daniel moving harder and faster, their passion reaching a pinnacle.

"You're amazing," Daniel told him breathlessly before taking his lips.

Robert clamped down, biting Daniel slightly. The coppery taste of blood touched Robert's lips. Lightning flashed again and the thunder rolled, adding still more energy to theirs. Robert vibrated with a power he'd never known his entire life. "Can't last."

"Don't." Daniel licked his lips and sucked at the base of Robert's neck, driving him further out of his mind. Another clap of thunder rattled the windows as pressure built inside Robert, the likes of which threatened to stop his heart. "Let yourself go. Don't worry about anything except your happiness. That's what I want to see." Daniel slid down him, drawing Robert's cock along his belly and hip.

Robert couldn't take any more and tumbled over the edge, his orgasm gaining control over his entire being. He clutched Daniel, feeling him shudder into release, their passions joining in breathless abandon.

The storm that seemed to have driven them both moved on, the thunder less sharp and urgent as it got farther away and more rumbly. Robert didn't move, enjoying Daniel's weight and solidity as he let his mind wander and float.

"I love this feeling. The afterglow, when everything is perfect."

"Nothing is perfect. I know I'm not."

"Yes, you are. You're perfect to me." Daniel seemed to know exactly what to say.

Robert chuckled, and Daniel looked at him like he was completely crazy. "I think I'm over my fear of thunderstorms." He buried his face against Daniel's chest, inhaling his rich scent, kissing his smooth skin with its hint of sweat.

"So you're saying…."

"That maybe when we were in New York, I should have jumped you at the top of the Empire State Building. Then maybe you wouldn't give a damn about heights any longer."

"Maybe if we had, I wouldn't have led us down this ridiculous path. It's obvious that we're more than business partners, regardless of what I might say with my big mouth."

"I like your big mouth, and maybe once we get up off this floor, I can figure out something pretty amazing for you to do with that mouth of yours."

"We'll just see about that." Daniel winked and sat up. "It looks like we made one hell of a mess."

Clothes were strewn around the floor and over cloth-covered furniture. The hamper had been kicked aside, and Robert hoped the contents were intact. He shifted and used one corner of the dustcover to wipe himself up. He felt like a naughty teenager who'd snuck in to have a bit of a romp.

"Why don't we get dressed and have some of the lunch you made for us?" Daniel wiped himself up as well and wandered bare-assed around the room, looking for his clothes. He found his underwear and stepped into them, dressing as he found other odd bits of clothing.

Robert dressed as well, meeting him, still disheveled, in the center of the sitting room. "We could simply pack up and go to a pub rather than stay here," he offered.

"It's still raining cats and dogs." While the one storm had passed, more lightning flashed and thunder neared once again. "I think we're going to be here for a while, so we might as well make the best of it. What comes to mind?" Daniel smiled and took a step closer.

CHAPTER 6

EVERYTHING ABOUT this relationship with Robert confused the hell out of Daniel. But maybe that was the attraction. When Daniel wondered what Robert had in mind to pass the time on a rainy day after they had blown each other's minds, he certainly didn't expect him to suggest that they check the upper floors of the house to ensure the leak had truly been plugged. But that's what they did, and things certainly seemed dry. The water-damaged bedroom now seemed dry at least, if still a mess. And afterward, while the second line of storms played out, they sat back in the sitting room they'd christened and ate lunch. Robert's eyes rolled and he jumped whenever the lightning got close, but Daniel did his best to comfort him and tried to take his mind off the storm.

Robert cleared his throat. "I don't think we should let what happened have any bearing on our business relationship." Robert looked down at the dustcover they were sitting on as they ate. "I mean, it really doesn't change things, does it?"

"Are you asking if, because I have feelings for you, that I might care for you, I'm going to run away and not do what I agreed?" Daniel shook his head slowly. "Is that an English thing? You fall for someone, so you screw them over and hurt them?"

"No. It's just that the more I think about the deal we made, the crazier it seems. And I care for you too, so I don't want to tie you to something stupid. I mean, really…."

"Look, it's a sound business deal. This place has a great deal of value, and I'm sure the land does as well. If we talked to some of the locals and maybe got an estate manager, someone who understands agriculture, and either leased out the land or worked it ourselves, we could make this place pay quite handsomely."

Daniel jumped up and pulled dustcovers off some of the furniture. Robert coughed, but that didn't deter Daniel in his rush. "Look at all this. These are beautiful antiques." He lifted one from in front of a painting on one of the walls.

"I know there's so much that needs to be gone through."

"You could probably sell some of the art to pay for the renovations, but that would diminish the collection, and that's one of the things we're trying to avoid. I went online the last few weeks and looked at the various places you can tour. With a few exceptions, most of them are overrun. They have more business than they can handle. With *Downton Abbey*, *Outlander*, and so many television shows set in the last two centuries... people just want to be part of it."

"So... what is it you're saying?"

"That we figure out how much it's going to take, get the work started, and try to generate some cash to keep the property going."

"But the whole marriage thing?" Robert got up, picked up the dustcover, and placed it over the chair once again. He paused there, his hands still, and Daniel wondered what was going on. "Bollocks, I have got to be out of my mind. Of course. My head is all muddled. We have to get married to protect your investment. This is an entailed property and, therefore, stays in my family. I could sell you part of the property, but then if something happened to me, the inheritance laws would kick in and convolute everything."

"So you're saying?"

"That if I married you, there would be some additional protection for you." His expression intensified, and Daniel felt a jolt of heat. "Look, before you put a dime into this place, I have to know that you understand what you're getting into. I won't have you doing something like this and get screwed."

"I know." Daniel grabbed Robert's arm. "That's part of what I like about you. You have integrity." Daniel realized he was the one who stood to lose in this deal, but they would both be taking risks. Daniel with his money, and Robert with the estate and his family holdings. "So let's not worry about things like that right now. What's more important is developing a business plan for the estate so we can figure out what we can do and start the work. The longer we delay, the more issues that will crop up."

"Okay." Robert became a little less edgy. "Let's clean up this mess."

Daniel helped Robert pack up the remains of their lunch and then put the hamper next to the front door. He opened it and peered out as the rain continued unabated. Maybe this whole thing was too much, and he should just go home. He could say all he wanted about being part of something older and needing a challenge, but whenever he thought of turning away and going back to his life in New York, something stopped him. He turned to Robert and felt a smile on his lips. Robert stood near one of the windows, looking out at the rain while he straightened his clothes. Daniel knew why he was interested in doing this, and it was Robert. There was something about him, something special that tugged at Daniel. He'd tried to deny it and hidden behind the idea that if they were business partners only, then he could walk away if he had to without getting hurt.

"I think the rain is letting up." Robert turned back to him, the soft light catching his eyes. It was just enough to see him, and Daniel sighed. This felt right, being here with Robert. But what he didn't fully understand why.

His phone rang, the tone echoing through the mostly shuttered entry hall, jarring him. Daniel clutched it, needing to make the awful noise stop. "Yes." He continued watching Robert as he spoke, not wanting to break the last of the spell that had descended over him.

"Daniel, it's Joanne. The Kick in the Pants warehouse system went haywire this morning. It specified that all orders be filled with the same boot and size. The warehouse team caught the error, and the technology team is working to fix it."

"Is there anything they need me to do?" Daniel's mind didn't want to make the transition from what he and Robert had just done back to his real life.

"They said that once the issue is fixed and the information rerun, they'll get people in and process the orders."

"I'll call the warehouse and talk to the guys there." Daniel started pacing. He always hated when things like this happened. Issues came up from time to time, but it was the ones that he couldn't help with that drove him crazy.

"I know you're pacing and you need to stop," Joanne said. "Things are in hand. You've only been gone a few days, and everyone knows what they need to do. I'm sending over some splash page designs for you to review and approve. I have another call coming in—I think it's the warehouse."

"Okay. I'll look for your e-mails, and call me once the warehouse issue is resolved."

"I will." She hung up, and Daniel put his phone back in his pocket only to have it ring again right away.

"This is Daniel."

"This is Nathan at the warehouse."

"Yes, Nathan. Are you still having issues?"

"That's just it. The system has started working again, and orders are coming through. I have people verifying them with the office to make sure they are correct before they get processed."

Daniel really did have an awesome team. "Great. I know things may run late, so fill what you can and bring in an extra team tomorrow if you need to. And be sure to order some dinner for folks who end up staying late."

"I will. I just wanted to let you know that things were working." Nathan said good-bye and hung up.

Daniel stared at his phone, and, of course, Joanne called back to tell him the warehouse issue was resolved.

"So how is your vacation going? Are things working out the way you hoped?" He heard her typing in the background.

"The house is beautiful. It needs a lot of work, and we're trying to figure out how we can turn it into a viable business." Daniel sat on the edge of a bench he'd uncovered, and Robert walked over from the window and motioned that he was going into the library.

"I'm not talking about that. How is it going on a more personal level?"

"I don't know," Daniel said as Robert left the hall.

"Have you given up this whole business-relationship thing?"

Daniel loved Joanne, but sometimes she reminded him of a mother hen. "I'm working on it." He smiled when Robert came back into the entry hall. "I've been working on it quite diligently today, and I like to think I'm making headway." He didn't take his eyes off Robert, and when he turned to pick the drop cloth up off the floor, Daniel's mind became clouded by the sight of Robert's pants tightening around his incredible backside.

"Daniel, are you listening?" Joanne asked, and he pulled his attention back to the call.

"I am now?"

"I asked… oh, never mind. Enjoy your holiday, and we'll handle things here. If there are issues, I'll call, and anything needing your attention, I'll send your way, but otherwise have a great time." She hung up, and Daniel put his phone in his pocket and was relieved when it stayed quiet.

"Everything all right?"

"Yes." Daniel put the warehouse issue out of his mind as well as Joanne's buttinskiness.

"The rain is finally letting up, so I think we can head back to the house if you like, and you could work for a bit if you need to."

"I will, but it can wait for a while." He helped Robert straighten the sitting room and recover the sofa before closing the door and walking back through the house. "We have things to do here."

"I think we've seen what we can for now. I have some people to call, and I'm hoping we can set up appointments for some expert advice on uses for the land. I know it could be subdivided and we could build homes on it." Robert sighed. "I really can't think straight with you doing that."

"What?" Daniel asked innocently.

"You looking at me as though I'm the main course at a buffet dinner." Robert stepped closer and Daniel pulled him near and kissed him hard, pressing Robert back against the wall and taking what he wanted. God, Robert truly did make the sweetest sounds, and they went right to his core.

"How about we go back to your place? I'm sure you have work to do, and I can try to catch up on things."

"I was pretty much able to clear my schedule for the time you're here. But I have calls to make to see if we can't get some things lined up." Robert didn't move. "You know, we should go."

Daniel stood still, looking deep into Robert's eyes. "I think I'm content to stay right where I am. After all, the view outside is amazing, but the one I have right now has it beat, hands down." Daniel leaned in once again, tasting Robert's lips, gazing into his expressive eyes.

"Mr. Robert?" a voice called from the front door, and Daniel backed away.

"In here," Robert answered, and Daniel tried to look as though he hadn't just mauled Robert, though if anyone knew what to look for, it would be plain. Robert's lips were puffy and there was a small mark on his neck.

Dicken came to the doorway but didn't enter. "Gene asked me to come up here and let you know that a tree fell in the storm, just outside the gates. It's an old one and it's blocking the way. It's going to take us quite a while to clear it. It's huge and we're going to have to take it apart piece by piece." He lifted the bag he was carrying. "Our mum sent some things over for you, and I can put it in the kitchen for you." He turned and looked across the hall.

"Thank you, Dicken. I appreciate you letting us know," Robert said, motioning toward his uncle's rooms.

"You could go out the back way, but I don't recommend it with your car. A Rover maybe, but yours is too low." He shifted from foot to foot nervously.

"It's all right. I appreciate you coming to let us know, and we'll take your advice and wait here until you can get the road clear. Do you need us to help?"

Dicken's eyes widened and he shook his head. "It's terribly messy work with the mud and all. If you can be patient, we'll set her to rights." He turned and walked away, and Daniel heard the door on the other side of the hall squeak open and then close.

"It looks like we aren't going anywhere for a while."

"Yeah." Robert checked his phone. "We may as well get comfortable." He turned to look around. "Let's go on through and see if there is anything to clean with. This place is so dusty, we should probably make one room habitable if we're going to be here for a while. Maybe the old study. It's small and just off the back of the hall. It also has a desk we can try to work at."

"Then let's get our things from the car." Daniel had packed his laptop and various chargers out of habit. Other than his phone and tablet, he hadn't expected to use them, but now he was glad for old habits.

"You do that, and I'll hunt up some things to make the place habitable." Robert headed toward the kitchen, and Daniel went out to the car with the hamper, dodging the now-sedate raindrops. He grabbed both his backpack and Robert's case, then carried them back inside and went through the hall to the open door and into the extremely masculine room, with its heavy woodwork, paneled walls, and large furniture. He carefully rolled up the dustcover on the desk and set it aside, then did the same with the covers on the chairs.

"This is unbelievable." Daniel stood in awe of the incredibly rich color and grain on the desk, with its still-intact leather top. He didn't want to touch it, let alone sit down to use it. He ended up in one of the chairs. He got a signal on his phone and turned on the hotspot connection before attaching his other devices.

"There isn't Internet out here, but…." Robert stopped when he came in the room.

"Just connect to my hotspot. I'll give you the passcode, and you'll be good to go." Daniel got up and took some of the supplies Robert brought in.

"I found a number of cloths."

"Then let's get started."

Daniel grabbed the broom, attached one of the cloths over the bristles, and used it to catch the cobwebs along the edges of the ceiling and around the coffers. Robert opened the shutters, swept the floors, and then wiped down the furniture. Once they were done, they carefully removed the dustcovers from the paintings and mirror. The hunting scenes that covered the walls were amazing, and Daniel looked at each one. He would have loved to be able to take hours to study them, but he had work to do.

"Someone was quite the collector."

"Yes. There is a room on the second floor with the estate records from when my first ancestor was awarded the estate by the crown. Every purchase is recorded and catalogued. I peeked through the room, but haven't had time to do all the research I'd like to. It will take months to go through everything and piece together what all is in this place." He finished sweeping and took care of the dust. "At least that's better."

Daniel put the dirty cloths in the box Robert had brought everything in and sat back down. "I don't think I've ever worked in more elegant surroundings." He smiled and brought out his tablet to start work.

After half an hour, the light through the windows dimmed and it started raining harder once again. "I don't think we're going to be getting out of here anytime soon. If this keeps up, the guys will lose the light in a few hours and then it'll be until tomorrow before we can get out," Robert said.

"I can think of worse things than to be stuck here in the estate with you. We can move to your uncle's rooms if we need power, right?"

"Yes, that should be the case." Robert settled in the other chair and stretched out his legs. "But who knows how long it's going to last. Those trees out by the road are very old, and if this rain and wind keeps up, we could lose another or the power could simply go. Out here, trees take the lines all the time."

Daniel checked the charge on everything, returned to his e-mail, and cleared it up as quickly as possible before opening his sales and production reports. Everything looked as good as he could expect, and when he checked on the warehouse, they seemed to be working double time to get the orders out before the shipping deadlines. "What does it feel like to be an earl?" Daniel asked, powering down his laptop to save battery. He figured he could use his phone and then the tablet if necessary, prolonging the batteries until they could get out.

"Not what I expected. I mean, in the movies, the earls and dukes have all the fun and spend their days being waited on and bowed to. They had power, and maybe if I had that I could do something with it. But this position comes with a title that's just that—a title. Nothing more. I didn't earn it, though I have people saying, 'Yes, my lord,' all the time. The guys at work do it to piss me off… and it does. But for me it's all fake. I have a house that needs so much work, it's pathetic, and an estate that's essentially broke. I could sell it all, and the tax people would take most of it and God knows what would happen to all this." He waved a hand, indicating the paintings and furniture.

"But you didn't know about any of it a few months ago. Why not just walk away, take the money, and run? That's what a lot of people would do."

"Yup. And if you drive through this country, there are tons of places like this that have fallen to ruin. They're only shells with walls and nothing more. The history and elegance is gone, taken by the elements and time because they weren't cared for any longer." Robert lifted his gaze. "This building survived the Blitz and all the bombs, it survived the Great Depression when no one had anything, and it's survived decades of my uncle's indifference. But if someone doesn't do something soon, all of it will end up as an empty shell. Because once the roof goes and the elements get in, it's the end of everything. And contrary to what anyone might think, who is really going to want to buy a white elephant like this? It needs so much work that buying it and fixing it up is too expensive. Not to mention, I can't really sell it anyway. So I'm the earl of nothing." Robert stood and walked to the window. "Sorry. I sounded like a whiny child. I know I'm luckier than most and there are plenty of people who would relish what I've been given."

"Yes, that's true. You've been given a healthy dose of responsibility, but choices as well. If you can make the estate pay for itself, then it can afford you a pretty elegant lifestyle. Think about it—you get to live in a home like this and there will have to be people to help you take care of it. There are many things you can have that most people can never dream of." Daniel motioned grandly.

"That's true." Robert turned back toward him. "You have plenty of responsibility to each of the people who work for you. How do you do it?"

"That's pretty easy. I don't think about it all the time. I'm a planner, and I make sure the business is solid with a plan for growth. I add people carefully and make sure each one is productive and helping to add to the success of the business. There isn't a single person in my organization who doesn't know how they contribute to the overall success of the business. That way we're all on the same page and working for the same thing. I have profit-sharing programs so that the more the business makes, the more my employees make. That gets them involved with the overall health of the business."

"So you don't try to do it all alone."

"Of course not. If I did, the businesses would all fall apart. I'm just the captain of the ship, but I have an amazing crew. You'll be the captain of this ship, and we need to find you the crew and experts to help you get it afloat again and sailing in the right direction. I think you already have a good start."

Robert sat back down and sighed. "It's just such a huge undertaking, and I wonder if I'm up for it. If I fail, I'll lose everything."

"That's not true." Daniel leaned forward. "Two months ago you didn't know about any of this. So if you try and fail, you'll be back to where you were before you inherited anything. Think of this as a business and keep it separate from the rest of your life and property if you can. In the US, we'd create a family trust of some sort and transfer everything to it. If the venture failed, then the trust would be defunct, but your personal property would be protected. I don't know if we can do something like that here, but as a barrister, I'm sure you can look into it."

"Not with this, unfortunately. Unless I were to turn the whole thing over to the National Trust, but that would mean handing over everything, and I can't do that. For one thing, my mother would be heartbroken. This is part of her childhood and it means a great deal to her, and regardless of anything else, this is a link to my past, my family history."

Daniel stood to stretch his legs, turning toward the windows. "I think I'm going to go on through to check out your uncle's living quarters. We're going to need to get something to eat, and it seems like the light is fading fast with this weather." He wasn't hopeful that they were going to get out of the drive tonight. While it wasn't that late, more thunder rolled in the distance, and that was certainly going to stop the guys from clearing the road. He hoped they'd already headed for shelter and weren't taking any chances. Daniel opened the front door and peered out. He could just see the pile of greenery on the other side of the gate. He didn't see any trucks or anything. The wind picked up, so Daniel closed the door once again before moving to the other side of the house.

Robert's uncle's rooms must have been in part of the building that had been damaged at one point. The rooms themselves were rather sparse and had clearly been refurbished in the last couple of decades. The walls were light in color and hung with various pictures, and the room was furnished with things that, were he to guess, had been bought in the early nineties. The rooms were small but relatively comfortable. He checked the power and was surprised to find it still on. He went back to the study.

Grinning, Robert was just hanging up the phone. "I got hold of a Matthew Duggins at the National Trust. He's going to come out next week, and he has a contractor that's worked on a number of properties that will come with him."

"Great."

"The information you gathered was very helpful, and I went over what we thought with him so he had an idea of what he was walking into."

Daniel smiled and began gathering his things. "The power is still on in your uncle's rooms, so we should move there and see if we can get comfortable for the night. We should probably look for candles, in case our power goes too."

"Maybe we should have gone there in the first place." Robert scanned the study they'd been using.

"Not on your life. If the rest of the house cleans up the way this room did, this place is going to be a stunner without a doubt." Daniel finished gathering his things and waited for Robert. He shut the door behind them and made a mental note to shake out the dustcovers and put them back over things before they left. "A good cleaning, some refreshed paint, and new curtains and draperies, as well as spreading the rugs again, would go a long way to making the house feel less...." He was at a loss for words.

"Like a haunted house."

"My thoughts exactly. Can you imagine how this is going to look tonight with the covers over the chandeliers? We could sell tickets and make a fortune scaring people out of their wits." Daniel chuckled, and Robert joined him as they went through to the more modern rooms.

THE STORMS and rain continued well past dark. Thankfully the power stayed on and they were able to heat up the shepherd's pie Dicken had brought. It was delicious, and with some bottles of water still in the refrigerator, they had a filling dinner.

"I found some sheets that weren't too dusty and made up the bed," Robert said as he rejoined Daniel in the kitchen area where he was throwing away the paper dishes they'd used. He was finishing up when the entire place was plunged into darkness.

Daniel stood still, afraid to move in the unfamiliar space. Robert's hands slid along his back and then around his waist. The storms outside intensified, with lightning flashing through the kitchen.

"God, I hate stormy nights like this. It isn't so bad when I'm home, but in a strange place…." Robert leaned against him, and Daniel felt him shaking.

He set down the plate and slowly turned around. "It's going to be all right." Daniel knew what it meant that Robert was willing to show his weakness in front of him, and he held him tightly while fishing in his pocket for his phone. He turned it on, and it cast enough of a glow that he could find his way out of the kitchen area and back through to the living room, with Robert right next to him.

They made it to the sofa and Daniel located the matches and a few candles they'd found earlier. He lit them and turned off his phone. The flickering light cast eerie shadows into the tall-ceilinged room. He tried not to think about it too much.

"What are we going to do?"

"There isn't much we can do. It seems like the storms are going to continue much of the night. So we might as well try to get some rest. In the morning we can figure out what's next." Daniel picked up one of the candles and handed the other to Robert, and they slowly made their way down the hall past the study and into one of the bedrooms. "Wait." Daniel turned and led Robert back through the modernish rooms and into the main hall of the house. "Think about it—this is how your ancestors would have seen this room at night, minus the dustcovers, of course. There wasn't electricity, so they would have lived by candles, gaslights, and lamps." The storm seemed to be strengthening, and Daniel put his free arm around Robert's waist.

"It looks completely different with shadows everywhere and the light being swallowed by the darkness in the corners. I can understand why they were afraid at night." Lightning flashed, shining briefly through the cracks in the shutters that covered the windows behind them. Robert tensed and his candle flickered when he jumped slightly as thunder rolled through the cavernous space.

"Yeah. I'm not going to take you through the rest of the house because you're already tense enough, but I thought this would be interesting." Daniel set his candle on the table in the center of the room, set Robert's candle next to it, turned to Robert, and kissed him. "Imagine all the places in this house where servants, gentry, and ladies all went to try to find a few minutes alone where they could do what people do best."

"You know, there were dire consequences for fraternizing. A servant would be fired without a reference, and if a lady was caught, she was ruined completely. Only the men got off scot-free."

"It was definitely a man's world." Daniel held Robert tighter as more thunder rumbled outside. "Come on. Let's go back." This probably hadn't been such a good idea. He handed Robert his candle, took him by the hand, and led him to the bedroom.

"Go ahead and get undressed. I'm going to get some water so we can rinse our mouths at least." He went to the kitchen and got one of the remaining bottles. They were going to need to leave soon or get more water. Hopefully the tree would be cleared early, and he and Robert could be on their way.

When he returned, Robert's candle sat on the bedside stand and he had the covers pulled up to his chin. The room had developed a chill that became more pronounced as Daniel stripped off his clothes. He blew out his candle and got in the bed. The sheets were crisp, but smelled a little like they had been in a closet for a while. The scent didn't seem too strong and would probably dissipate quickly. "Are you okay?" Daniel asked as he turned onto his side.

"I will be."

Daniel tugged Robert to him, sliding until he'd spooned right behind him. With the storm and all, Daniel didn't think tonight was a good time to get amorous, but his body seemed to have other ideas.

"Daniel." Robert's voice sounded small and unsure.

"Yeah?"

"Make love to me."

Daniel's mouth went completely dry. He tried to remember the last time those words had been used in reference to him, and he could come up with only one time... and that was a memory he didn't want to think about. Theodore had asked him to make love to him, and that had been just a few weeks before the end, when everything, including Daniel's heart, had shattered into a million pieces.

Robert must have sensed Daniel's hesitation. "If you don't feel up to it or you aren't interested...."

Daniel tightened his hold on Robert, burying his head in his shoulder, trying not to let the memory those words invoked spring forward. Robert wasn't Theodore, and Daniel needed to stop the association before it went too far. "I think you can feel just how interested I am," he said. "It's just that I haven't heard those words in a long time."

Robert rolled over, and with a single flash of lighting, his gentle face illuminated and took Daniel's breath away. "I've never asked before."

Daniel heart squeezed and then leapt. He tugged Robert closer, running his hands up his back and neck, cradling Robert's head, guiding him closer until their lips met in a moment of blind ecstasy. The more he learned about Robert, the more he got under his skin. "I don't have anything with me and I won't hurt you." Daniel cut off what he was certain was going to be Robert telling him not to bother with such things.

The storm built once again outside the massive stone walls, rolling through them and into the bedroom. Like before, Daniel used the energy and let it wash over them, holding Robert and taking them both to heights he'd only been to before a few times in his life. As lightning flashed and thunder crashed, they reached the pinnacle of desire, and as they tumbled into the abyss, Robert screamed his passion at the top of his lungs, adding it to the fury of the storm and letting it carry it along in its wake.

ONCE HE fell to sleep, Daniel slept like the dead and woke to sunshine streaming in the dirty windows. It was nearly blinding in its brightness, and he got up and pulled the curtains closed before returning to the bed and Robert. He'd rolled away from the light, his hands under his head, still asleep after their exertion.

Daniel lay back down, dozing until he heard a banging and realized it must have been the front door. Daniel slipped out of bed. After putting on his clothes, he padded barefoot to the door and peered out. "Morning, Gene."

"Do you have power? The village took a lightning strike and it zapped the power. We have it back."

"Then hopefully we will too. How is the tree situation?"

"We're already working to get the last of it cleared. It should be an hour."

"Thank you all. It's much appreciated." He was about to close the door but stopped. "Is there anyone in the village that you think could do some heavy cleaning?"

"Of course. Mrs. Mullins used to work at the park some years ago. She was a housekeeper here before she got married."

"Perfect. Can you see if she'd like a job cleaning this place from top to bottom? Windows, floors—the works. If she has people to help her, that would be fine too. You know what it looks like, and we need to start bringing it back to life." He gave Gene his phone number. "Call me directly and I'll arrange to get everyone paid for their time."

"What does the earl think of this?"

"It's a surprise for him," Daniel said with a grin, imagining the look on Robert's face once the house had been put to rights. There were days of work for multiple people in the house, but it would be worth it to see the end result.

"Thank you. I'll let you know what I find out."

Daniel reached into his back pocket and pulled out three twenty-pound notes and handed them to Gene. "Have a few drinks at the pub tonight on us. You deserve it." He pressed them into Gene's hand with a smile and closed the door. Then Daniel returned to the bedroom where Robert was still asleep, burrowed deeper under the covers in the cool morning air that came in through the window Daniel had cracked earlier. He sat as gently as he could on the edge of the bed and watched Robert sleep for a few minutes. He was beautiful, his mouth open slightly, fingers grasping his pillow.

"What are you doing?" Robert groaned softly without opening his eyes.

"Just sitting here."

"You're watching me sleep."

"Maybe." Daniel gently pulled back the covers and stroked Robert's shoulder. "The storms are over and the sun is shining. Gene said they'll have the tree cleared pretty soon."

"Then why are you not back in bed?"

"Because I thought we could look around the grounds before we left."

Robert groaned. "I'm tired, and with all the storming, I was up for part of the night."

"Okay." Daniel leaned over Robert, kissed him lightly on the shoulder, and got up to find his shoes and finish getting dressed. Then he left the room and went outside to the car for his light jacket. After putting it on, he headed out along one of the narrow roads that led away from the house.

He walked awhile, looking at the landscape as he passed. He wondered if there had been any formal gardens around the property. What he saw were grand trees and large lawns that led the eye in every direction. He crested a slight rise and stopped as the landscape around him spread to the horizon in spectacular beauty. The trees must have been a hundred years old, some towering to the sky, others smaller and budding with stunning color.

A figure approached up the drive he'd taken, and as he watched, Robert drew closer.

"I thought you were going to sleep some more."

"You weren't there." Robert walked up to him and then turned, looking where Daniel had been. "It's an English lawn park. From what I saw in the records area, there weren't large formal gardens, but the area around the house was planted with these large vistas in mind. Of course everything has gone a little wild, but I think I like it. There isn't the fussiness of intricate plantings, just the beauty of nature."

"Yeah, I know." Daniel concentrated on the house. "It looks like it's been there forever."

"In a way it has been here forever. Mum told me the stone is that color because it came from a local quarry that is now played out, pretty much. She said her father got some stone for repair purposes and that there is some of it still on the property somewhere. I love the yellowish color in this light."

"It looks like it's alive with the sunlight." Daniel put an arm around Robert's waist. "I think I could be very happy here. *We* could be very happy."

"Are you serious?"

"Yeah. I really think so." Daniel pointed to the house. "There's plenty to be done, but could you imagine spending our days making that spectacular again? And being able to come here whenever we want to look out over our home?"

Robert turned toward him. "You're really serious. You want to live here… with me."

"I think so. We could bring this place back to life and then share it with the world." Daniel pulled his phone out of his pocket, snapped a picture, and then forwarded it to Regina with a note. *Ashton Park. Robert and I are thinking of making it amazing again.* He sent it, and his phone chimed seconds later.

It's beautiful, Boo Boo. I take it things are going well with Robert. Tell him I'm looking forward to meeting him.

Daniel read the message to Robert, minus the Boo Boo part. *Robert says he's looking forward to meeting you too.* Daniel sent the message and lifted his gaze away from his phone. "By the way, that's code for grilling you to check that your intentions are honorable." Daniel grinned.

"I expected as much."

His phone chimed again.

I take it there's room enough for me to come visit.

Of course, though the guest rooms are a little rustic at the moment.

Ha-ha! Be careful and I love you, Boo Boo.

Daniel groaned and shoved his phone in his pocket. "I wanted Regina to see what we were seeing. Sorry for the interruption."

"Of course you do. I can't wait to meet her, grilling and all." Robert turned his gaze back to the view.

Daniel spun slowly around to take in the whole view. "What are those?"

"Outbuildings of some sort. Mum said there were workshops and garages. At one time there was a greenhouse to supply the house with fresh flowers, but I suspect that's long gone." Robert moved a little closer, his hip pressing to Daniel's. "So you're thinking—"

"That the wild and totally improbably scheme of ours might be working out for the best. I know we talked about getting married and all that. But I think instead of jumping in feetfirst, we should finalize our business relationship, and then continue to work on the rest. I think we have plenty of time to figure out if we truly want to spend the rest of our lives together as earl and count. What do you think? We give ourselves a break and make sure we truly want 'till death do us part.'"

Robert sighed. "You have no idea what a relief that is."

Daniel wasn't sure of he should be insulted or not. "O-kay."

"I didn't mean that in a bad way. Just that decisions made in haste are usually the wrong ones." Robert looked up at Daniel. "But what about the reunion?"

"I won't be a count, but I'll be the fiancé of an earl. That should give the snobs something to talk about." Time was flying, and the reunion was just over a month away.

"If you're sure. Thank you. I'd really like your help with the house, and for now we'll remain officially engaged until we decide to take it further."

Daniel thought that was best. "So how do we seal our bargain?" He wriggled his eyebrows.

"Smart-arse."

"I didn't say anything."

"Fine, then—smart-eyebrows." Robert grinned, and Daniel tugged him tight. "After last night, there's only one thing I can think of. But considering I don't want to take any chances that someone will see your bare arse out here, I think this will have to do." Robert leaned in and kissed him.

"You know," Daniel said once Robert pulled away. "This could become the new way of sealing a deal. Instead of shaking hands, people kiss."

"Yeah, could you see Theresa May kissing Angela Merkel to seal a deal?" Robert teased.

Daniel clamped his eyes closed and shivered. "I have to get that image out of my head. Ewww."

Robert laughed and kissed him again, driving the offending image from his mind and replacing it with a flashback to the night before when they'd made each other scream at the top of their lungs. Now *that* was truly the capstone on a bargain.

CHAPTER 7

"THANK YOU so much," Robert said and hung up his office phone two days later. He messaged Daniel saying the people from the National Trust would be able to meet them at Ashton Park the following day. Robert had made it clear that he wasn't interested in donating the property, but that didn't seem to matter.

"Our primary mission is to preserve our history, and we can help support you," Matthew Duggins had told him, seeming excited. "We've had our eye on Ashton Park for a while, hoping that someone would do something with the property before it's too late." On the phone he had seemed like a serious but happy man who loved what he did, his passion for preserving British history apparent in every word he spoke.

Great :) Daniel responded to Robert's text.

Robert was supposed to be working on a case that he was preparing for court, but his mind wandered to him and Daniel. Since that night at the estate, they'd continued to sleep together. Well, they had been in the same bed for the last two nights, but Robert wasn't sure exactly how much sleep they'd gotten. He smirked to himself and yawned.

A knock on his door pulled him out of his thoughts. "Are you all right?" When he looked up, Blake came in and set a file on his desk. "Here's the information you asked for."

"Thanks." Robert tried to stifle another yawn and failed.

"I'll bring you a cup of strong tea." Blake smirked. "Your lordship."

"Don't be a smart-arse." Robert picked up the file but didn't open it. "Is there something else besides picking on me?"

"Nope."

Robert had come to learn that that smile said something different. "What?" He needed to try to get back to his case before his client ended up losing her home.

"You've been different. Smilier." Blake continued to stare.

"Okay. Well, thank you for that report." Robert turned to the file and read through it. "This is good news." He continued reading and smiled. "Send a note to opposing council and explain that they are going to want to meet with us. It seems they missed something."

"Okay. I know that 'cat that caught the canary' grin." Blake came in, closed the door, and sat down. "That's the expression you get when you're about to win a case. But the other, sappier smile that's been pasted on your face is new." Blake put his hand over his mouth. "Are you in love?"

"I don't recall you butting into my personal life as being part of your position."

"It is. I added it last week." Blake wasn't going to be put off. "Come on. I know I'm your assistant, but I'm also your friend, and you know you couldn't live without me."

"Break into song and you are so out of here."

Blake laughed. "I don't sing in the office." He leaned forward, his eyes widening. "So am I right? Are you in love? Because you know, if you are, that's the greatest thing ever."

"I don't know." That was as honest an answer as he could give. Robert wanted to believe that things between him and Daniel were progressing, and yes, Robert was most definitely developing feelings for Daniel, but he wasn't sure if they were in love or what. He hoped Daniel felt the same way he did. Robert shook his head to clear the wandering thoughts. He needed his mind on his work and not in the clouds. "Don't you have anything better to do?"

"Not really."

Smart-arse. "Then do you need me to find something for you to do? I understand that the ladies have been complaining that the cleaning crew isn't doing a good job in their loo." He held back the smirk as Blake's smile fell and his lips contorted into a look of near horror as he jumped to his feet.

"I know you're kidding, and I already called them to come back out and finish the job." Blake scrambled for the door and turned back with a grin. "Don't think I'm not going to be keeping an eye on you." He left his office, leaving the door open, and Robert went back to work.

And if he stayed smiling longer than was necessary, that was his business.

"YOU'RE A little later than usual." Daniel placed a bowl of salad on the table. He'd taken to cooking the last few days and seemed to delight in having dinner ready when Robert got home. Robert knew he had no right to expect it, but he could get used to being taken care of like that pretty easily. "Your mother is on her way over. I made more food than I needed, so I invited her to join us." Daniel and Robert's mum got along amazingly well.

"Let me get cleaned up." He put his case on the chair near the door. "Does Mum want me to pick her up?"

"No. She said she wanted to walk."

Robert quickly washed up and returned to find Daniel lifting the lid on one of the pots on the stove. Steam rose and the room filled with the scent of herbs, garlic, and tomatoes. Robert's stomach rumbled as he tried to remember if he'd skipped lunch. "It was really busy today, but I was able to clear my calendar for tomorrow, and I even got a head start for later in the week." He'd purposely tried to lighten his schedule for the time Daniel was here. He'd been hesitating about asking when Daniel thought he'd be able to come back. "How are things back home?"

"Good. I had a creative team meeting this morning, and we're thinking of adding some boots based on English traditional designs. I've noticed that the boots are a little different here, and I think they'd catch on if we promoted them."

"You've been looking at people's boots?"

"Of course. Find out what people like, add some style and flair, and you have a winner. And with our technology for making custom boots, I'm going to look into setting up a subsidiary somewhere in Europe so we can get direct access to the market."

"Only you would spend two days looking at people's boots."

"I've done more than look. While you've been at your office, I've been in mine. I've been to three pubs and had pints with guys, asking them what they wear to work, what they liked about their boots, and how much they'd like a pair that was made just for them that didn't cost much more than the ones they were buying now. I also got a few names of factories here that supply boots for their employees that I'll see if I can do business with. There's a whole untapped market here. We have shipped boots to Europe, but the cost is high. Producing them here will cut a lot of that excess cost and make them more affordable." Daniel looked like a kid in a candy store. He practically bounced around the kitchen. For Robert, seeing him that happy added to the success he'd had as well.

There was a soft knock and then Robert's mother came in the back door.

"Isabelle," Daniel said, walking around to kiss her on the cheek. "I'm glad you could join us."

Robert kissed his mother as well and guided her to a chair. In the five days he'd been there, Daniel and his mother seemed to have hit things off in a big way. "The National Trust is coming next week to help us assess Ashton Park." He really hoped there wasn't some major disaster lurking under the surface.

"We're mocking up potential budgets for the work that needs to be done, and I found an arborist who will meet us as well." Daniel grinned. "It seems Gene is a wealth of information, and one of the men who used to garden at Ashton still lives in the village there and will walk the property with us."

"I see you've been busy," Robert's mum commented.

Daniel set the dish of pasta on the table, and Robert got three beers and handed them out before sitting.

"What about the house in London? Have you made any decisions about that?" His mother took a little salad and then passed the bowl to Daniel.

"I think we're going to tackle one property at a time. The London house, while in need of work, is sound and closed up for now. It can stay that way until we can get to it." Robert had talked it over with Daniel and figured one thing at a time was best.

"There's also a Mr. Harkins—"

"Tommy Harkins?" his mother interrupted.

"Yes. Gene said that he used to work on the estate and that he knows about crops. He worked for the agriculture office after leaving Ashton, and I thought we might talk with him as well."

Robert heard what Daniel said, but it was his mother who had him fascinated. "What is it?" He took the salad Daniel passed him, though his focus was on his mum.

"Tommy Hawkins cut quite a swath when he was younger." She blushed slightly.

Robert took some salad, set the bowl down, and then got some of the pasta. Damn, it smelled so good. "Did he turn your head?"

"He turned the head of every girl for twenty miles. Tommy Harkins was a hound dog. And I wasn't going to let him sniff around me. Papa would have had a fit. But I always thought he was nice, and he most definitely had a way with animals. I remember a skittish lamb that had lost its mother. She'd been killed, and Tommy cared for that lamb until it was old enough to be on its own. That little orphan lamb ran from everyone, but not Tommy. He had a way with them."

"Did you want to come with us when we meet with him?" Daniel asked, and she nodded.

For some reason Robert wasn't so sure about that, but since she seemed excited about the prospect, he kept his opinion to himself. "Do you really think these people can help us?" Robert asked. "I mean—"

"Yeah, I do. It isn't going to hurt us to listen to them, and they all know Ashton Park. Your uncle pretty much shut the place down and did nothing. We could take what was done back then, modernize it, and make it pay. Doing things the way they did in the past isn't going to do us any good, but learning from what's been done can keep us from making the same mistake and help us learn from their successes."

Robert nodded, feeling a little left out, he guessed. Daniel was a ball of energy, and while what he'd done sounded good, he'd gone ahead and made appointments without discussing it with him. Robert knew he should be grateful he didn't have to do everything on his own, and Daniel was only asking that they meet with various people who could help them. He hadn't made decisions about what they were going to do, but it rubbed him the wrong way sometimes.

"Don't get your knickers in a twist." His mother glared at him and then turned to Daniel. "In case you haven't figured it out, he's a little peeved, probably because you didn't talk to him first."

"Mum...."

She faced him again. "Well, you are. You were always about controlling everything, and you can't with something like this. My father ran Ashton, but he had an estate manager, gardeners, and household staff. He trusted them, and you have to trust the people you're working with." She turned to Daniel and then back to him before taking a bite of her pasta. Apparently his mother was done embarrassing him for the moment.

"I...." Robert sighed and snagged some pasta onto this fork. "I guess maybe I'm a little scared." He couldn't look at either of them. This was just too hard to say with someone looking at him straight on. "This is a whole lot of responsibility, and I'm really wondering if it will be worth it. I mean, it all sounds so noble to say that I'm repairing Ashton Park for the next generation, but there isn't going to *be* a next generation unless I have children, and I'm a little shy in the ovary department." He knew he was being flip and that there were other methods, but he was trying to make a point. "So what if I simply walk away from this and just let it go?" His own doubts were getting bigger and bigger, and had been for much of the day. He hated questioning himself like this, but it all seemed to be coming out now.

"I was only trying to help," Daniel said. "If you don't want me to do anything, then that's fine. If you've changed your mind and want to do this alone, that's fine too. I'll pack up and go back to my business in New York." Daniel was clearly hurt, and Robert failed to see how to undo what he'd apparently done.

"No." Though he argued in front of some of the toughest judges in the country, he was at a loss for words because he knew whatever he said had the potential to end something important almost before it really got started. "It's my doubts coming forward." Maybe this wasn't the best time to be having this conversation. "I just wish you'd have talked with me."

"I just did. I was out doing some research and I ran into Gene and his brothers at the pub near the estate. I bought a round of drinks, and he introduced me around, and before I knew it, I had a crowd of people all wanting to tell me what Ashton Park meant to them." Daniel set down his fork with a gleam in his eye that Robert didn't understand. "They shared stories about working there in the old days and how things were, and they talked about how Isabelle's father used to let them wander the grounds when their work was done. Did you know how many people met their husbands and wives at Ashton Park and then courted them on the grounds?" Daniel paused. "If this is going to be a success and we're going to be able to bring the estate back to where it was in its glory eighty to a hundred years ago, then we're going to need more than you and me. The community support will go a long way."

"I guess I never thought of that."

"You're a lawyer, and a good one, judging by the people here in town that you've helped. Those people sing your praises down at the pub and are proud that you're the new Earl of Hantford. They wish you only success, and they can't wait until the house is open so they can come to visit. They're an hour away and they know about it. Some of them have driven over just to see it because it's your place and they care about you."

Robert swallowed hard.

"So they just want to help, and if we use their expertise, it'll make them feel included. And once we open, we'll have hundreds of people talking about Ashton Park rather than just you and me. There's a mason here in town who'll do some of our work. His father helped build the gates to Ashton Park and he still has the original designs."

Robert was completely bowled over. Daniel had found out so much in only a few days. "But… what can I do to help?" He felt so insecure with things like this.

"Well, maybe after dinner, we all go down to the pub, buy a round for the house, and talk to people. You were saying that you wanted to go through the estate records. People there will give you a living history. They're your neighbors and friends." Daniel picked up his fork once again.

"Okay." Robert had never really thought much about friends and being popular. He certainly wasn't in school, so he'd worked hard and kept his head down. He knew he'd helped a lot of people in the area, but he figured once his job was done, they went on with their lives and pretty much forgot about him. Maybe he was wrong.

"This is what I do," Daniel continued. "Yes, I had the initial ideas for the businesses, and lots of people have ideas. I'm good at taking those ideas and making them a reality. I did it for both the apparel and boots, and I saw what Regina could do and helped her set up her design business."

As he took another bite, Robert waited for what else Daniel had to say. It was strange, but he hung on every word.

"So when I went into the pubs originally to talk about boots, word had gotten around that I was the fiancé of the Earl of Hantford. Some of the guys stayed away until the others came forward, and then I was just one of the guys and they opened up."

"I can never do that."

"Sure you can. So you're a barrister and an earl. If you treat them like just one of the guys, they'll treat you the same way." Daniel reached over and took his hand. "I'll go with you, and you'll have fun. That's the name of the game."

"All right."

"And once you make friends with these people, who knows what you're going to learn?" Daniel flashed him an excited grin and continued eating. "Do you want to come, Isabelle?"

"No. I think I'm going to let you boys be boys. I have a good book that's calling to me for when I get back home. But I would like to come meet this man from the National Trust with you."

Robert shared a gaze with Daniel and then agreed. "You know the house."

With all that settled, Robert finished his dinner and beer, happily full. He cleared the table, and his mother took charge of the dishes.

"You boys go on. I'll finish here and walk home. The exercise is good for me and it's a nice night."

"Are you sure?" Daniel asked, and she shooed them out the door.

Robert walked him toward the center of town and the Crown and Castle, a pub that looked like it had been there since the conquest. He'd seen it many times, but for some reason, he'd never been inside. It was a working-class place, and he'd never felt like…. It was strange how he'd never felt like he belonged there.

He pulled open the door and stepped inside after Daniel. The ceilings were low, the walls and tables wood, darkened with age and the touch of generations. "There's a table over by the wall." Robert moved in that direction, but Daniel stopped him with a light touch on his arm.

"What can I get you, Danny?" the barkeeper asked.

"Give us a couple of your best beers, and share some with the rest of this lot from the new Earl of Hantford." Daniel clapped him on the back.

The barkeeper turned to Robert and extended his hand. "Nice to see you, my lord."

"It's Robert, please." He shook his hand.

A cry went up at the bottom of the pub where a group of guys were playing darts.

"You lot. Come and get a pint and shake hands with the Earl of Hantford. He's buying."

The conversation grew louder and the drinks were passed out. He expected people to thank him, and they did, but after that, they went back to what they had been doing. Robert was at a loss. He'd hoped someone would talk with him.

Daniel grabbed him by the hand. "Have you played darts before?"

"Yes, I—"

"Who will challenge the earl here?" Daniel asked the group of dart players. "I understand he's quite good."

All of the men stood back, making room at the board. None of them approached, and Robert was beginning to think this exercise was a total bust.

"I will," a man in his early twenties said as he stepped forward.

"Henry," one of the other men half hissed, but Henry waved him off.

"I'm Robert." He shook Henry's hand, and Daniel passed out the darts. "Go ahead." Robert was a terrible dart player, and he demonstrated just how bad he was on his first turn when he only hit the board with one dart.

"My lord, that was…," Henry stammered.

All the men stood, watching as though this were some royal display. Robert had never experienced something like this. The entire scene struck him as ridiculous. "Please. I'm so bad at this game that anyone outside should fear that I'm going to throw one through the window. Why don't you all go back to playing?" He set his darts on the table and stepped back. "Go on, lads. I don't want to impede your fun. Now cricket...."

"You play?" one of the men asked.

"I used to until I hurt my knee a few years ago. But I adore the game. Do you lads have a team?"

"We play every Saturday," Henry told him. "Come and watch sometime."

"I will." Robert smiled, and the conversation around him shifted as he spent the next hour discussing cricket with everyone. That little snippet of information seemed to break the ice and Robert was surrounded.

"I understand you're going to fix up Ashton Park," Henry said once the conversation lulled for a few seconds.

Robert could talk cricket for hours, but was glad for the change in subject. "I'm going to try. Daniel and I are forming a partnership of sorts to try to bring it back to life."

"The old earl was a real putz."

He didn't see who said it, but it came from one of the men to his left. Robert had to agree. His uncle hadn't been a very good steward of what he'd been given.

"People are who they are, putzness and everything. And I'll endeavor to keep my own putzness to a minimum." He reached for his glass, and the others held theirs up in a sort of toast.

After that, the barriers seemed to fall. Robert was inundated with men asking him about the estate and the older men telling him stories. Ashton Park was nearly an hour away and he hadn't dreamed that its influence would extend so far away, but it obviously had, at least to a degree.

"How are things?" Daniel asked once most of the men had gone back to darts. The novelty of having him there had worn off.

"Good." Robert shook hands with Henry as he said he was off for the night. "See you later." He turned back to Daniel. "I think I'm ready to go too."

"Do you want me to handle the tab?" Daniel reached for his wallet, but Robert stopped him with a touch, approached the bar, and paid the tab, leaving some extra.

"Good night, all!" Robert called, and received waves and good wishes in return. Then he and Daniel stepped out into the night. "I never realized."

"Because you had no way of understanding just how far the reach of the estate is. If we complete this project, there will be jobs for people. Some will work the land for us, and others will be needed to maintain and keep the buildings. There will be ticket sellers and tour guides. I see twenty or thirty people being involved, and that means food on the table for some families."

"How do you know all this?"

"I've been reading and I understand commerce. These estates used to hire large staffs, partly because they needed the labor, but also because the estate was a major source of work and employment in the area. Their staffs were often bloated. They were make-work institutions." Daniel took his arm, holding it. "Ashton Hall has been sitting empty, and the effect of reopening it and making it a viable enterprise will not only help the community there, but skilled people will find work from as far away as Smithford. So yes, there is responsibility as you said, but there is also a greater benefit." They made the turn onto his road and continued to his house. "I guess I wanted you to see that what we're going to be doing is bigger than just a building or a family legacy."

"Okay. I think I get that now. But why are *you* doing it?" Robert stopped, and they stood in the middle of the road in near pitch-black, with only the light from a few house windows to illuminate the area around them. "Is it just because of the title?"

"It stopped being about titles quite some time ago. Yes, my reunion is coming up, and I'd love it if you went with me. But… I thought that showing them… up, I guess… was really important."

"You show people up by being who you are, and if they only respond to some pedigree, then they aren't worth bothering with." Robert leaned in and kissed him as a car approached. They parted, chuckling to each other as they got off the road and let it pass. Then they continued on to the house.

"I have hundreds of people who work for me, and each of them works hard. They rely on me to run the business as successfully as I can so they can be secure in their jobs. These people here want the same things. Let's just say that I'm understanding that there is so much more to having a title and living up to that title than I ever imagined."

Robert stopped outside his front door. "Don't you get it? You live up to one every day, even if you don't actually have one. You don't think of Kick in the Pants as your business or your accomplishment. Yes, you own it and run it, but it's something more than that to you. You think of it as a group effort and look at the business as more than the bottom line. It's—"

"It's part of me, and I hope it's part of each of the people who work for me. And I think Ashton Park could be the same for you."

"And you?"

Daniel paused, and Robert waited for his answer. "Yes. I think in time Ashton Park could become part of my soul, just like the man who owns it." Daniel reached around him to open the door. They half stepped and half tumbled inside. Robert got the door closed and was up against it in a matter of seconds. Daniel pressed to him, chest to chest, his lips demanding, devouring, driving him higher, teasing and taking. It was heady, and Robert clung to Daniel so he didn't slide down the wood onto the floor.

It was so easy to lose himself when Daniel got like this. The urge to let Daniel take control was nearly overpowering.

Daniel slipped his hands down Robert's sides and tugged his shirt up.

Robert quivered at Daniel's firm touch. "I think we need to go to the bedroom." Robert gasped for air, and Daniel cut him off again, taking his lips. Robert wound his arms around Daniel's neck, holding on. He laughed against Daniel's lips when Daniel lifted him off his feet. "I can walk."

Daniel held him tighter and set him down. Once he was steady, Robert took Daniel's hand, led him back to the bedroom, and kicked the door closed behind him. He only hoped that he didn't wake the neighbors.

THE FOLLOWING morning Robert was scheduled to be out of the office, so he let Daniel talk him into spending the day over at Ashton Park. The plan was to speak with Gene and his brothers, as well as some of the people Daniel had met at the pub.

Robert unlocked the door and steeped inside. "What happened?" He wondered if he'd stepped into the wrong house for a few seconds. The woodwork gleamed and the dustcovers were gone. Paintings hung evenly throughout the entryway. "My God."

"Yeah."

"Did you do this?"

"Yes. Some of the ladies in the village used to work here, and they brought some people with them. They spent the last two days going from top to bottom. All of the rooms have been given a thorough cleaning and dusting. The rugs have been unrolled and are lying mostly flat again. Some of the edges may curl, so be careful."

Robert walked into the library and then the dining room, the ladies' parlor, and the game room before returning to the massive library. The woodwork gleamed, and light flood ِd in through huge windows that were so clean, they sparkled. The shelves were still empty, but he didn't mind. "You brought it back to life."

133

"It was hidden under all those sheets and layers of dust. There are some repairs that will need to be made. Dicken has said he can make some of them if we want, but he thinks the ones in here should be completed by an expert. Some of the others are just some light water damage in a few spots on the ceiling. He thinks they're dry now and will check if the plaster is solid. If it is, he can match the paint color. If not, he'll leave it until we can get a proper plasterer."

"My God." Robert stood with his mouth hanging open.

"There are a number of places where paintings once hung that are empty. I'm hoping they're in storage with the books." Daniel smiled. "But I found something you'll want to see." He walked over to the desk and gently opened the top drawer. He pulled out a photograph and handed it to Robert.

"Is that who I think it is?" Robert lifted his gaze to Daniel in near disbelief.

"Yes. I believe that's Queen Victoria standing in this very room. And there are other pictures in the desk. I bet there might be an album somewhere with the other records possibly, but this is awesome. We could include a picture gallery of sorts—a record of people who have visited. It would add to the visitor experience."

Robert nodded as his attention returned to the library. "I can't believe you did this."

Daniel bit his lower lip. "After spending the night here, I realized how dreary it looked, and I thought it might give you a lift if the rooms were cleaned and the dustcovers removed. It's an impressive house, and the rooms are stunning. We'll have to have the curtains remade. The ones that are here aren't in the best shape, but we can use them as patterns."

"So you did this for me?"

"Yeah. I wanted you to be able to see what you were working toward."

"I guess this is a bad time to tell you that I hate surprises." Robert kept his lips pursed for a whole two seconds and then grinned. "This is so awesome." He went through all the downstairs rooms and then up to the bedrooms. They were less impressive because the beds were bare and the mattresses gone. "I suppose they had to throw out what was here."

"Yes. They were covered but decades old. They were modern and not historically significant. We'll get new ones, and for a few of the beds, have custom mattresses made. The one in the master is an odd size, and I don't think we want to alter the bed."

"No." Robert wandered into the bathroom and rolled his eyes. This was where the manor really showed its age. A few of them could probably be repaired and saved, but the rest were a mess, with tiles falling off the walls. "I suppose the men from the National Trust will be able to give us some advice."

"I suspect so." But Daniel smiled anyway. "I think this house can be spectacular."

"I'll admit I wasn't seeing it before. All I saw was the work and the mess and the money it was going to take to do something, and—"

"Yes, it will take money and work, but this is what's waiting underneath it all." Daniel cocked his eyebrows, and Robert fell a little more in love with the man. He had that ability to understand what Robert was missing, that he wasn't understanding. And what did he do? He helped him do just that by showing him. He took a little action and made Robert's day.

A motor sounded outside. Robert stopped and then went to the window. "What is that?"

"A lawn mower. The grass has been left on its own, and that stops as well. The area around the house will be cut and trimmed almost back to the trees. It'll take some time to thicken up again, but it will. It's time the estate be treated as though it has value rather than with neglect."

"You sure don't let grass grow under your feet."

Daniel lowered his head and looked up from under his lashes. "Are you mad? I figured these were little things that we could do to make the place more presentable."

"You're right, of course. But where did the mower come from?" Robert continued looking out the window.

"Gene's cousin has a gardening service. So he's renting the mower, but we'll need to buy our own equipment eventually. For now, though, everyone is making do, and we don't have a huge cash outlay." Daniel smirked at him when he turned away from the window. "I also thought it would help make an impression on the National Trust people."

Robert supposed it couldn't hurt. "What did you have planned for today, besides your surprises?"

"A visit to the pub for lunch and some research and community outreach. Maybe we can take a look through the estate records."

"Okay. I've been doing some digging myself, and the more historically prominent a location can be deemed to be, the easier it is to get the tax deferrals we need." Robert checked his watch and turned to leave the bathroom. "We have a couple of hours. The records are down here." He led the way to the end of the hall and opened a door near the back stairs to the servants' area.

A single small window at the far end provided the only light. "I'll be glad when we can have the wiring checked out and then we can turn the power on to the entire building."

"Aren't you optimistic."

"It never hurts." Daniel stepped inside and instantly began to sneeze. He stepped back out and continued sneezing for a few minutes before the attack died down. "Jesus. I don't know why that happened." Must have been lingering dust in the air.

"Yeah." Robert dove in and looked over the shelves of record books and ledgers. He wasn't sure where to start.

Daniel seemed to zero in on a slanted cabinet worn dark by decades of hands and plenty of ink. He opened the drawer and stared down into it. "We need to get some gloves for the stuff in here. These look like some of the plans for one of the expansions of the manor. There are line drawings and goodness knows what else in here." He waited for Robert to take a look and then closed the drawer again. "I don't want to damage anything, but we can probably conserve them and add those to the history exhibition on the estate."

Daniel had so many ideas, it was sometimes hard for Robert to keep up. But for the first time, he was excited about the prospect of what they were doing and was enjoying working with Daniel. Daniel got him excited, in more ways than one, and some of the worry that had been weighing him down had lifted without Robert realizing it until now.

After finding gloves, he settled in to review the earliest records, with Daniel standing next to him. As they looked through the books and papers, his shoulder touched Robert's every now and then, and Daniel would share a soft smile before returning to what he was doing. They worked side by side in near silence, but Robert was attuned to each move Daniel made. It was special to have that kind of connection with someone.

"Did you—" they both said at the same time. Daniel motioned him to go first.

"Did you find anything interesting?"

"Yes." Daniel carefully set down the small book he'd been looking at. "One of your ancestors was a history and genealogy buff. Someone put together this first part of your family going back to what looks like a relative of Henry II. I'm not sure how accurate this early history is, but there are a great many details in the last five hundred years that are likely to be more realistic. Here's your mother and uncle, but nothing has been added after that."

"I wonder if this is true and that we're related to the royal line." He couldn't help smiling.

"Many people are. It's estimated that if you trace back far enough, as much as 10 to 20 percent of Americans are related in some way to the royal family, so it has to be true here as well, especially among the landed classes."

"You sounded so English for a moment."

"I think I'm picking up the local lingo." Daniel picked the book up, closed it, and placed it where he'd found it. "What have you got?"

"A ledger for Victoria's visit. She stayed for just two days, and the visit cost nearly forty thousand pounds from the look of it. Of course, there was all the preparation, and then the food and entertainment. I bet the earl at the time was relieved to see her go." Robert closed the ledger. "I think that's enough for today." His nose itched, and from the way Daniel's eyes were reddening, they both needed to get out of the dusty room. Daniel hadn't wanted this room cleaned until everything could be gone through. "A beer and some lunch might be just what we need."

Daniel helped put the books and ledgers they'd gotten out back where they belonged, and then they left the record room and closed the door. "You seem happier now," Daniel said. "Even your walk is light and springy."

"You watch me walk?" Robert asked.

"Of course. There's a reason why I follow behind you when we climb stairs." Daniel leaned closer. "The view is amazing."

Robert colored and felt his cheeks heat. "I thought I was the only one."

"Nope." Daniel raised his eyebrows. "I watch you all the time. I know when you're angry because your eyebrows grow closer together. I know when you're really excited and just about ready to come because your eyes sparkle like a pond when it catches the first morning light. And now I know what 'happy' and 'carefree' look like. You smile and there's a bounce in your step." Daniel slid an arm around his waist and pulled Robert to him. "And that tight little butt of yours goes up and down in the most amazing way."

"Daniel…." If he kept this up, they were never going to get to the pub. But Daniel buried his face in Robert's neck, nipping lightly and making Robert shiver. "How do you make me feel this way?"

"Like what?"

That smart-arse. Still, Robert shivered when Daniel sucked at the base of his neck. God, he wanted this more than food, more than a beer, even if his throat felt like sandpaper—maybe more than air at this very moment. He cradled Daniel's head, running his fingers through his silky hair and closing his eyes, giving himself over to such a simple pleasure as being adored. That's what this was. Robert knew exactly what this was.

Growing up, his mother had cared for him and loved him always. But this was different and special. As Daniel popped open each button on his shirt, smelled his skin, and caressed each inch of what he exposed, Robert shook harder. He leaned back against the hall wall, hands splayed against the cool plaster. It was different and mind-blowing. Daniel parted his shirt and pushed it off Robert's shoulders. Robert groaned softly, but Daniel seemed to be in no hurry, each movement deliberate and slow as his fingers drew swirls and arcs over Robert's skin worthy of any modernist painting.

"Daniel…" was all he managed to gasp as his knees shook.

"You smell warm and clean, like the fresh air outside." Daniel pressed his cheek to Robert's belly, inhaled, and then gently caressed his side.

"I do?"

"Yes. Like grass after a long cool rain. You make me want more." Daniel grabbed his arse and squeezed firmly.

"You can take whatever you want."

"No. Not here and not now." He pulled away, running his hands up Robert's belly before settling them on his chest. "I'm not being a tease, but you deserve so much more than a quickie in a hallway." Daniel pulled him closer. "There will be plenty of time once I get you back home for me to have my way with you."

"So what was this?"

"Just a little quiet time." Daniel leaned in and kissed him with care and gentleness. The heat was there, banked and warm rather than searing, but Robert knew it would flare to life and burn hot and bright once Daniel was ready to release it. Eventually Daniel pulled away, extending his arms until his hands fell to his sides. But he didn't look away for a second. Even as Robert brought his shirt back into place, he felt Daniel's gaze on him. "What did I ever do to deserve you?"

"I don't know. Maybe hire a matchmaker and show up for a date in New York. Remember?"

"You did the same thing."

"See, we're both a little crazy, so maybe that means we're meant for each other." Robert buttoned his shirt, but Daniel stopped him when he went to tuck it in.

"Loosen up a little." He took Robert by the hand and led him to the entry hall. They locked up the manor and headed to the pub. "We're going to have a little fun and meet some more people."

Robert was hungry as heck. It was well after one in the afternoon when they passed through the gate. Daniel closed it after them, and then Robert drove toward the village. He'd never really paid much attention to it, but the homes and businesses were old and looked in need of some care.

"This is a poor area with few jobs. Most people either work someplace else or are pensioners. Opening the house and bringing in visitors is going to help the entire area," Daniel said.

Robert continued the drive to the pub and pulled into a parking slot alongside the road. He'd opened his door when Daniel's phone rang. He wasn't sure if he should wait or not, but Daniel motioned him on, intent on his call.

"What?" Daniel snapped rather loudly. "No way in hell." He pulled the phone away and reached back into the car to get something. Robert knew that tone and it couldn't be good. Daniel noticed Robert hadn't gone in yet. "I'll be there soon." He smiled, and Robert went inside the Ashton Park Arms.

The place wasn't as old as the pub from the night before, but it still had an air of age and contentment. Mostly men sat at the tables or the bar, eating their lunch and having a pint.

"Can I help you?" a man asked, coming around the bar.

"I thought I'd have some lunch. My mate is still outside, but he'll be in." He was going to buy a round, but didn't think it would do if people had to go to work.

His host looked him up and down. "You aren't from around here."

"Not originally, but I will be pretty soon, I guess."

"Did you buy the Gartner place? I'm Horace." He held out his hand, and Robert shook it.

"Robert. Glad to meet you. And no, I'm afraid I'm not who bought the Gartner place." He hesitated to say who he was, but he was being examined so suspiciously. "I guess the plan is that eventually I'll be moving into Ashton Park."

"Crikey, you're the new earl? Then the mate you're waiting for is Daniel." He grinned. "Chaps, stand up and meet the new Earl of Hantford."

"Please, it's Robert." He sat at a table near some of the other men. They didn't meet his eye, and Robert knew he needed to break the ice. Just as he was figuring out how to do that, Daniel came inside, his face stormier than the night they'd been stuck at Ashton Park.

"Hey, guys," Daniel greeted, but the warmth was forced. The others didn't seem to catch it, but Robert did as Daniel took a seat next to him.

"What can I get you?" Horace asked.

"What's good for lunch? Fish and chips?"

"Always."

"Then bring us two." Daniel motioned Horace to come closer. "And give his lordship here the tabs for everyone. Today, lunch is on him."

Horace looked at him and Robert nodded. Horace hurried off, and Robert turned to Daniel.

"What's going on?"

Daniel sighed as his phone rang again. He stood and walked to a quieter part of the pub to answer it. Robert watched as his cheeks got redder. He couldn't hear what was being said, but Daniel's posture grew stiffer and he started to pace. The tension in Daniel's body was so strong, Robert could feel it, and his own breathing shortened.

He heard Daniel's tone rather than the words and then saw Daniel look over at him, his expression completely unreadable, but it still sent a chill up Robert's spine. Something was very wrong. He wanted to go up to him and wasn't sure if he should. Then Robert figured, what the hell? If the other people in here were offended or bothered by the fact that he was gay, then they could take a flying leap. Robert stood and walked to where Daniel was listening to whoever was on the other side of the line. He placed his hands on Daniel's shoulders and felt his muscles relax under them.

Daniel turned to him without putting the phone down, gave him a nervous smile, and leaned his head against Robert's for only a few seconds, but it was enough.

Robert returned to his seat and realized every single set of eyes in the place was on him. After a few seconds, the conversations around him started up once again. He knew he was here to talk to people, but Robert wasn't in the mood. All his attention was on Daniel and what was happening. He couldn't think of anything else.

Eventually Horace brought two huge plates of fish and chips. Daniel ended his call, still flushed, his lips pulled into a straight line. He sat and began to eat. Robert caught his eye, and Daniel tilted his head toward the door and then dug in. Robert knew they'd talk later, but not in here.

Robert ate his lunch and kept looking over at Daniel for a clue as to what all those calls had been about. He knew it wasn't good. The gleam that had been in Daniel's eyes before—even while he'd been sneezing his brains out—was gone, and nervous energy fizzled in the air around them both. He barely tasted his food at all.

"How is your lunch?" Horace asked, standing way too stiffly.

"It's great, Horace. Thank you." Robert motioned to the chair, and Horace looked around before pulling it out and sitting. "I don't want to stand on ceremony. Yes, I'm the earl, but I'm really Robert, a bloke like everyone else. And your fish is some of the best I've ever had."

"Thanks, your… Robert." He looked so uncomfortable.

"I was hoping to be able to spend some time listening to people's stories about the Park, but we need to cut our visit short. I'll be back for sure." Robert handed him some money. "Is that enough?"

"Of course." He took the bills with shaking hands. "The next time you come in, the beer is on me."

"I'm looking forward to it." Robert stood, and Daniel followed suit as his phone rang yet again. Robert let him step outside while he said good-bye to everyone. By the time Robert left the pub, Daniel had hung up and stood leaning against the car, even more agitated than before.

"I have to go back to New York."

"Right now? I mean—"

"Blake is chartering me a plane, and I need to get back to your place, pack, and go right to London. There's a company, Heartland Shoes, that wants our technology, and they're trying to buy the company… out from under me."

Just like that, the happiness Robert thought was building popped like a soap bubble.

CHAPTER 8

"I'M SORRY, Robert," Daniel said when he got a few minutes to catch his breath before the meeting started. He'd talked to Robert every day, though most of the time it had been late at night or early in the morning, and Robert had been so understanding through all of it. "You deserve so much better than this." He sighed. "I've been in meeting after meeting for damn near two weeks, cajoling and convincing people who should have had my back in the first place to take my side on this. Heartland's executives are nothing but corporate bloodsuckers, and if they get hold of Kick in the Pants, there will be nothing left of it. They'll take what they want and either sell or close the rest." The thought of them taking his dream apart was too much.

"So it isn't going well."

"No. I have a board meeting tomorrow. They were able to convince the venture capital firm that their bid should be placed in front of the board and shareholders. Then they purchased shares privately and have gotten others on the wagon with promises of a huge payout. It's taken all of my extra cash to try to shore up my position." Including the money he'd earmarked for investment in Ashton Park. Daniel had already told Robert about it and felt like a complete heel.

"What time is the meeting?"

"Eleven at the offices." He was so nervous because he really wasn't sure if he had enough votes for things to go his way. Never had he thought he'd lose control of his own company. "I'll call you and let you know how things go. And I'm sorry for all of this."

"It's not your fault." Robert sounded anxious. "I'll let you go. I'm thinking good thoughts."

Daniel wasn't sure if they would do any good, but he was so glad he had Robert's support. It meant more than he'd ever considered.

"As you say, knock 'em dead." Robert ended the call, and Daniel set his phone on his desk and began making more calls.

"HOW CLOSE are you?" Joanne asked as she came into his office at the end of the day, clearly concerned. Daniel had tried to keep the entire mess from the rest of the company. Whatever happened, he didn't want them to feel threatened. If he lost, Daniel would personally explain what was going on.

"So close I can taste it. But not quite there, and I don't know who else to speak with or what else I can do."

"Then go home. You know all the shareholders very well, and if they've deserted you for a quick payout, then they don't know what they're doing."

"I like to think so, but the money Heartland is throwing around his hard to resist."

She placed some files in his desk. "These are the printouts you asked for, and I organized them so you'll be able to find what you need quickly."

Daniel stifled a yawn. "Go on home. There isn't anything more we can do tonight." He locked his computer and put the reports in his bag to go over at home.

"Are you okay?"

"Yes. Just go and have a good night. We're going to have to be on our toes tomorrow. So please get some rest."

She wished him a good night. "Don't stay up half the night."

"I'll try." He finished packing his things and left the office a few minutes after her.

When he got home, he flopped down on the sofa, called for delivery, and thought about calling Robert, but it was late here, which put it too early over there. Robert was surely in bed, and he didn't need to wake him up when there was nothing Robert could do to help.

Daniel spent the next hour reviewing the reports he'd asked for, and he found nothing in them that would help. He just needed one additional vote to put him over the top, but he wasn't sure where he was going to get it. At this point all he could do was hope that someone changed their mind or that he could persuade them at the meeting itself.

His Chinese food arrived and he went down, paid the delivery man, took it back up, and ate as he stared at the television. He never thought he'd lose out on something that he'd built from scratch—his *idea*, his *dream*. He'd come up with the concept that was making the company so valuable, and someone else wanted it and thought they could come in and take it. It made him angry as hell, but got him no closer to a solution.

Eventually, he went to bed and tried to sleep, but mostly he tossed and turned for a large part of the night, checking the clock until it was time for him to get out of bed. Thank God for adrenaline and coffee or he wasn't going to make it through the day.

He got to the office, and rumors were swirling like crazy, most of them inaccurate. Not that it mattered. Daniel had to concentrate on the task at hand. He made his notes and went over the paperwork he had one more time.

"Daniel." Joanne knocked on the doorframe. Her expression showed complete puzzlement. "There's someone here to see you." She leaned in the office. "He's really cute and has a really sexy accent. He says he simply must see you."

"Please have him make an appointment." Daniel didn't care how cute Joanne thought anyone was, he had to keep his head in the game.

She stepped back and turned around. "You can go right in."

"Joanne...." Daniel was about to raise his voice when Robert stepped into his office. Daniel got to his feet, unable to believe his eyes.

"You're welcome," Joanne said as she closed his door.

"What are you doing here?" Daniel's feet carried him around the desk before he thought about it.

"I couldn't let you go through this all alone. I know what this business means to you. You built it and nurtured it from nothing into something wonderful." Robert lowered his gaze, and Daniel followed it to the boots he'd given Robert. "They are the best pair of shoes I have ever had on my feet. They were made for me, and they feel like I'm being cradled. When you were there with me, I felt like I could do anything, like you had my back, and now that… all this has happened, I can't let you go in there without me having yours."

Daniel felt the strength ooze out of him. Robert was right there, holding him up and letting Daniel be weak for a little while. It felt good to know that he didn't have to be strong all the time, that Robert would be there when he needed the support.

"What's the plan for today?" Robert asked.

"Well, first is a board meeting, and Heartland is going to try to get the board to take the vote to the shareholders. If that succeeds, and since either the shareholders or their representatives will be there because the stock is closely held, there will be a vote to sell the company. The thing is, Heartland has been working the board and the shareholders, so I don't know if I have the votes in either case. Right now I know I control 49.5 percent of the voting shares…." He sighed.

"What is it?"

"Nothing. It's pretty much out of my hands now."

"So you think you'll win?"

"I have to see how this plays out."

"Where is the meeting going to be?"

"The board will meet in the large conference room near where you came in. Joanne is probably setting it up already." He checked the time and his heart beat faster. "Go in there with her and take a seat off to the side. Shit… only stockholders will be allowed to be in there…. Go get Joanne and have her come here right now, please." He excitedly dug through his paperwork once again.

Robert seemed confused but did as he asked, seeming to know Daniel needed to get this done fast.

When Joanne hurried in, Daniel said, "I need you to draw up a document saying that I sold one of my shares of Kick in the Pants to Robert Morton, Earl of Hantford, today, right now. Robert, do you have a dollar?" He held out his hand, and Robert gave him a five.

"It's all I have from my last trip here."

"Thanks." Daniel took it and placed the bill on his desk. Joanne hurried away and returned with a document, which Daniel signed. Then he handed it to Robert, who also signed it. "Now you can be in the meeting."

"Speaking of, I need to finish setting up for it," Joanne said and left the office.

"Will one share make a difference?"

"No. But you will be asked to vote the share."

"You didn't have to do that. I could have waited."

Daniel shook his head. "No. I need you there." For the last two weeks, he had been on edge, jittery, not sleeping, and he thought it was the whole mess with Heartland, but when Robert walked into his office, Daniel immediately felt better. Everything came into sharp focus, and what was truly important was clear.

"Okay. I'll go see if I can help Joanne and let you do what you need to. I'll see you in the meeting." Robert turned to leave, then walked to where Daniel stood, watching him, and cupped Daniel's cheeks in his hands. "Go out there and don't let these bastards steal your dream away from you."

"That's just it," Daniel said. "I started this company and everything I have because I had some good ideas and thought others would like them. I built this entire company up from nothing. And yes, it was my dream, but it isn't any longer. I have new dreams now." Daniel held Robert's gaze. "So I'll survive whatever happens."

Robert leaned in and kissed him hard. "I don't think I've ever been anyone's dream before."

"Then get used to it." Daniel smiled and leaned his forehead against Robert's. His mind was clear, and he was content to see this through. "I need to make one last phone call and then I'll be in."

Robert backed away as Daniel snatched up the phone.

DANIEL WALKED into the conference room half an hour later and closed the door. His call had taken a little longer than expected, but he was exactly on time. Daniel shook hands with each of the board members, whom he knew well, he'd thought.

"Let's get down to business," said Harlon McGuire, one of the directors Daniel knew was firmly in his corner.

"Yes. I think we have a few things to discuss." Daniel went to the head of the conference table. The others were sitting, but he didn't. "I started this company six years ago, and we opened Kick in the Pants eighteen months ago. All of our divisions are doing remarkably. We hit our five-year goals in two, and then the next set of goals a year after that. This company is healthy and will remain so"—he leaned forward—"as long as we don't let people like Heartland rape us for our ideas and innovations."

"This is a business, Daniel," Coreen Lofton said. She was one of the venture capital firm representatives on the board. Daniel liked her, and she had always been a great source of advice.

"Yes, and it's *my* business with *my* ideas, blood, and sweat poured into it, along with that of every person who works for us. This isn't about me or about making a fast buck. It's about being a part of the community. Heartland is going to take what they want and the rest will disappear."

The meeting room was quiet.

"Daniel—" Coreen turned to Robert, who sat along the wall. "—why is he here?"

"This is Robert Morton, eleventh Earl of Hantford, and he's a shareholder and my fiancé." He tried not to smile and nearly failed. That idea made him too damn happy for words, but this wasn't the time to show it.

"Very well." She turned to the group. "The topic of discussion is the sale to Heartland. Since there is deep division on the board over this matter, I make a motion that the decision be put to the shareholders."

Daniel had expected discussion and debate, but the directors all nodded their heads, seeming resigned to letting it be decided in that manner. "All right. Since that's your decision, please call in the representative from Heartland and let's get this done." Daniel wanted to put this to bed.

Carl Hanning got up from the other end of the table and opened the door. Phillip Wilson came in and walked through the conference room, presumably to shake Daniel's hand.

He had no intention of touching the man at all. "Take a seat over there and we'll call the role and vote our shares." Daniel turned to the board secretary, Gregory Young, who had the list of shareholders.

"I don't have the earl's sale recorded," Gregory said.

Robert handed him the page Daniel had given him earlier.

"Thank you." Gregory nodded that it seemed in order and made no indication if he thought it strange that Robert had only one share. He then called the list of current shareholders, and they expressed their vote.

As they went around the table, it became clear to Daniel who was on his side and truly shared his vision for the company, and who didn't. There were no surprise swings in his favor like Daniel had hoped would happen. He voted his shares, and Robert voted his one. Then he waited, glancing at Robert, who surprised him by standing and moving next to him.

"We can't let this happen. I'll sell what I have to in order to stop this." Robert squeezed his fingers and let go quickly.

Daniel smiled. He appreciated the gesture more than he could say. Robert truly was his partner.

"With all but one shareholder voting, neither side has the majority," Gregory explained.

"Yes," Phillip said. "The last shareholder is Voices for Children, the charity that was given 1 percent of the company at its founding. We have been in touch with them, and they have agreed to sell. So here is…." He made a show of pulling out a sheet of paper.

Daniel squeezed Robert's hand. That was it, then.

"May I see that list of shareholders?" Robert asked, and Gregory handed him the printout. Daniel wondered what Robert was looking for. He seemed to scan the list. "Gregory, did you confirm the voting status of all the shares?" Robert turned to Daniel and lowered his voice. "I know you have a huge heart, but you aren't going to put yourself at risk if you can help it. When you gave this charity the stock, you did it so they'd have the revenue. But did you also give them the voting rights as well?"

Daniel gasped. In all the hubbub, it had completely slipped his mind. "No, I didn't. I retained the voting rights to those shares." Daniel wanted to kiss Robert right there. "Gregory, you need to confirm."

"I already am." He had his laptop open and was typing away as tension and anticipation built until it nearly caused a fog. "You retained those voting rights." Gregory nodded to Daniel.

"So that 1 percent votes to reject the sale. I believe that's enough and the sale is defeated." He glared at Phillip. "Which concludes that order of business."

"Then I believe we're done," Coreen said.

"No. We are not. This board is still divided, and I will not run this company with a board I cannot count on. Therefore, I am calling for the immediate election of discretionary board members."

"Excuse me?"

"That's right, Carl." He looked around the conference table. "I want resignations on my desk by the end of the day, or you will be removed from the board. I need people with vision and integrity, not merely a love of what is quick and expedient. And our first order of business will be the repurchase of the shares owned by Heartland... at book value." He turned to Phillip and saw him pale.

"You can't do that."

"Yes, I can. Check the bylaws." Daniel walked around the conference table. "Don't you ever start a war you can't win. Now get out of here. This company is not for sale."

Phillip stormed out, the door crashing closed behind him.

"Are there any questions? If not, this meeting is adjourned."

As certain directors quickly left, Daniel stayed where he was as some others approached him.

"You were magnificent," Coreen told him. "And I can guarantee they won't be back."

He wasn't sure what to say, since the venture capital firm had voted to take the offer. He quirked an eyebrow.

"Don't you worry. I'm going to straighten them out."

He nodded and thanked her as other directors came to shake his hand, even some of those who represented people who hadn't agreed with him.

"You won," Robert said, grinning.

"He did more than that," Coreen interjected. "Regardless of what anyone thought before, he handled this in a way that told everyone he wasn't someone to be messed with, and that will go a long way." She patted him on the shoulder. "We'll talk next week about the details of the stock repurchase." She excused herself and headed for the door.

"And about a European expansion." He saw her pause for a second before leaving the conference room.

"That was a thing of beauty." Robert smiled.

"I had forgotten about the voting rights on those shares. It was recorded and official, but I'm glad you pointed it out. Otherwise this would have turned into a bigger mess."

"So what now?" Robert asked.

"Let's celebrate with a nice lunch." He turned to look at Robert.

"Not at the Plaza," they said together and then laughed.

"Come on. Let's get out of here." Daniel had been through the wringer and he hadn't slept well since he'd left England. The fight was over, and he'd prevailed. But at a cost. The cash he'd had available to put into Ashton Park was gone. He'd needed it to buy shares from a wobbling investor. In the end he owned more of his company, but it meant his assets were less liquid and that cash wasn't going to be as readily available for a while. Daniel led Robert to his office, and Robert closed the door for a little privacy.

"I've thought about it, and I can borrow the money against my shares in order to allow us to continue with the Ashton Park project."

"You'll do no such thing." Robert practically growled.

Daniel sighed. "I have a small amount I can use to buy in, but not what we originally planned. And you're going to need it to get things started. What are you going to do?"

"We're going to take your investment and start on the most critical items on the list. Mainly the plumbing and electrics. You've already paid for the roof to be repaired, and as long as we don't have a winter that's too harsh, we should be able to make it through with what we have until the other work is done. And by then we should be able to open the house for tours and events to start bringing in money."

"I thought the roof was a loss? What about the gutters?"

"The house has limped through on what's there for twenty years. We'll try to make sure it can for a few more. It's our only choice." Robert got a grin that was so sly, Daniel wondered what he was up to.

"See, it so happens I'm marrying this very smart, wealthy man who owns and runs an Internet company, and he's going to help me."

"What a coincidence, because I have this fiancé who's some sort of earl or something."

Robert grabbed Daniel's arm. "I think it's time we made this official." To Daniel's surprise, Robert knelt down slowly, holding his hand. "Daniel, you are a magnificent man. You take care of me and others without thinking twice about it, and always seem to do the exact right thing. I know we started our relationship in what has to be the weirdest way possible...."

"Robert...."

"Daniel, I know what I want, and I don't want a business relationship with you. I want more. I want you to hold me during thunderstorms and make me wonder if the shaking I feel is from the thunder or the pounding of my heart."

"Are you really sure this is what you want?" Daniel felt the same way, but he had to ask. He'd stopped acting in a businesslike way with Robert a long time ago.

"Yes. I want more than business between us. I want you to be my husband and the Count of Hantford, and I want to be Mr. Internet Sensation. I know it will take some time and travel. You'll be here part of the time and with me in Ashton Park at other times, but you are who I want in my life."

Daniel choked up and wasn't able to answer right away. "Yes. But I want to make it clear that I'm marrying Robert Morton because he's a pretty awesome man and the one I fell in love with. The Earl of Hantford can come along for the ride." He tugged Robert up and kissed him hard, and it took him only a few seconds to remember he had glass walls on his office and everyone outside could see him. The catcalls started within seconds, and Robert pulled away and blushed beet red. "Sorry," Daniel whispered.

Robert took his hand. "Okay. I know we've called each other our fiancés because of our earlier agreement, but for the first time, I feel like it's true."

Daniel understood the warmth that settled inside. He liked it and never wanted to be without it. "Come on. Let me feed you, and then I'll take you back to my place and I'll show you exactly how it should feel."

Robert's eyes glistened and he swallowed hard.

They left the office hand in hand. "Joanne, I'm going to be out of the office for the rest of the day. I've done my world-saving act and that's enough for now."

"So is it official, official?" she asked.

Daniel glanced at Robert, and they both nodded. Winning the fight for his company had been heady and made him want to mock-punch the ceiling. But this was even better. "Yes. It's definitely official. Send out the announcements and call the papers. Robert and I are going to get married." He rolled his eyes at the ultragooey look she gave them.

"Have you set a date?" She was clearly getting the wedding happies.

"Not yet. But when we do, we'll be sure to let you know so you can plan the whole thing." Daniel turned to Robert. "I see a wedding in Central Park. And when we're in England, we'll stay at Ashton Park. It's going to be one of our homes."

"Is that where you want to live?" The hope in Robert's voice was palpable.

"Of course. We can make it a home again." At least that was what he hoped. The business here hadn't changed, but he was going to be watched going forward, Daniel had no doubt about that. The venture capitalists who owned part of his business hadn't been the people Daniel had thought they were or the ones they had originally professed to be.

"Daniel, are you still with me?" Robert asked, pulling him out of his wandering thoughts. "We were talking about Ashton Park."

"Yes. I want to make it our home, along with the one here in New York. You need to decide what you want to do about the house in London, but that's up to you. I can't live there permanently with the business here, and there are all kinds of immigration laws to contend with for both of us, so I thought we'd keep a place here for when we came for business, and Ashton Park will be our residence when we're in England. Is that okay?"

"What about my practice?"

Daniel didn't see the problem. "What about it?"

"If we live at Ashton Park, then I'm an hour away from my office. And I don't want to give it up."

"Then we'll live in Smithford if you don't want to commute." Daniel shrugged. He thought Robert wanted to live at Ashton Park and wasn't understanding the issue. "You think about what you want. Ashton Park is going to need someone to oversee and manage the property. It will need someone to deal with the people we hire and to see that all the various things we want to do come to fruition. Whether I'm in England or here, I'm still going to need to run my businesses." He squeezed Robert's hand. "These are things we can give some thought and work through. We don't have to have all the answers today."

Robert nodded his agreement, but Daniel could tell there was definitely more talking they needed to do. "I guess I thought that you'd be the one to run Ashton Park."

That floored him. Daniel was willing to help and support Robert, but his plate was already full. "I can't. I don't have the time, and I'm not the earl. You need to be the one to take the reins and manage it. It's your ancestral home." He looked around. "Where are your bags?"

Robert waved toward Joanne's desk, Daniel used his phone to call the car service to let them know he was ready to be picked up, and they left the building.

"But I want to keep my practice." Robert closed his eyes. "I guess I have some decisions to make after all."

"You don't have to make them alone." He hugged Robert slightly. There wasn't much Daniel could do for Robert at this point other than listen and be supportive while he figured out the direction he wanted to take his life.

The car approached and pulled to a stop in front of them. They got inside, and Daniel told him where to take them for lunch, but most of the celebratory mood seemed to have vanished. Honestly, Daniel had figured that once this issue was resolved, it would be smooth sailing for them. They still had things to work out, but obviously they had both made assumptions that could turn out to be incorrect.

"There is a solution," Daniel offered. "Open a second office in Ashton Park village. Your partners would work on Smithford and you could work in Ashton Park. No commute, the people near the estate would have access to top-notch legal services, and you could continue to practice law and run the estate if you wanted." It sounded so logical.

"You have all the answers, don't you?"

"I try. I want you to have what you want." Daniel didn't understand the shortness in Robert's tone. "It was only a suggestion. You can do whatever you like."

Robert exhaled deeply and slumped on the seat. "I guess I want it all and I can't have it. I want my old life and the new one too. How can I help the people most in need and then come home to a house like Ashton Park? Most of my clients have nothing at all and are being taken advantage of."

"Who better than you to help them?" Daniel glanced at the window briefly and then back at Robert. "I know you don't like the trappings that come with your new title. The 'my lords' and things like that. But you're the Earl of Hantford. Who is better equipped in many ways to help them? Your title has influence, and you don't need to go to court to get things done. Yes, you may come home at night to Ashton Park, but you'll be able to use the influence of your job, as well as your office, to make things better."

"I hadn't thought of that. Maybe because I've been trying to keep the parts of my life separate."

"I don't think you can. Your life is a whole—my job, your job, your positions. I think you need to integrate them all." Daniel squeezed his hand again and Robert squeezed his in return.

They pulled to a stop, and Daniel opened the door, waiting for Robert before heading into the restaurant for their lunch. The mood seemed to have shifted, and Robert smiled and was happy. Daniel loved that smile, especially the way the lines reached to his eyes.

"You feel better?"

"Yes. I don't know what I'm going to do yet. I have some thinking and decisions to make, but they shouldn't cast a cloud over today." He took Daniel's hand, rubbing small circles on his palm. "A few months ago, I never would have guessed just how my life could be turned upside down and sideways."

"Maybe. But do you really regret it?" Daniel thought Robert had such a huge heart. "I mean, your uncle doesn't seem to have been a very big-hearted person." He took the menu, then set it down again and looked Robert in the eye. "You can make the earldom strong again and have it mean something. There's no one I know who'd do a better job at that than you."

THEY WENT back to his apartment, but instead of racing to the bedroom, they settled on the sofa. It was amazing to hold Robert in his arms and be together again, but something wasn't sitting right. He should have been over the moon. He had won his battle for the company, and Robert had actually proposed to him for real and not part of a business arrangement.

"Is it okay if I take a nap? I'm so tired after the flight. I was actually supposed to be here last night, but it was delayed and I didn't arrive until a few hours ago."

"Of course." Daniel would have gone with him, but his phone rang.

"Take the call. I'm really tired." Robert stood and went toward Daniel's bedroom.

Daniel watched him go as he grabbed his phone and took the call.

"How did it go, Boo Boo?" Regina asked with way too much energy.

"Well, there's lots to tell. We're not selling, and there are going to be some changes on the board. I need people who understand my vision, and some of them clearly don't."

"Okay."

"Robert flew over. I wasn't expecting it, but he came to support me." Daniel's heart warmed whenever he thought about it. "He also asked me to marry him, for real, because he loves me."

"That's great." The line buzzed a little and then the sound dissipated. "So why are you talking to me rather than celebrating?"

"Because there is so much up in the air." He told her about their conversation regarding where they were going to live. "I told Robert he could live wherever he wanted."

"Sometimes men are so dumb." She sighed. "Can I ask you something? Robert is potentially moving his law practice, or part of it, to Ashton Park so you can live there. He might sell his home and move because he knows you'd love to live there."

"Yes. It makes sense."

"Does it? He'll be living there essentially alone when you travel for business, and I think you said last week when we were arranging for me to let you vote my shares that his mother lives close to where he does now."

"Just down the street. They walk to visit each other."

"So it sounds to me as though you're asking Robert to make all the sacrifices. I know you don't have the cash you were hoping for to put into Ashton Park to get the work going at the moment, and you and Robert want to move into Ashton Park and make it your home. So what sort of sacrifices are you planning to make for him? Do you love the guy?"

"Oh yes." He turned to look toward the bedroom. "He's amazing and I couldn't imagine not having him in my life." How that happened in such a short time surprised him.

"Then you need to figure out what you're going to do to show him. Relationships require devotion, and you can't expect him to be the one to give up everything."

Daniel stared blankly at the wall of his apartment. "You're right. If this is going to work, then I need to support him. Thanks, sis. I can always count on you to hold up that mirror, flaws and all."

"It's my lot in life, Boo Boo. I have to go. I'm being summoned, but call me and let me know how things work out." She hung up, and Daniel set his phone on the counter.

He found Robert in the bedroom, eyes closed, looking as beautiful and quiet as Daniel had ever seen him. Daniel took off his shoes, walked to the far side of the bed, and sat next to him.

"Is your call done?" Robert mumbled, and Daniel lay down beside him.

"Yes. It was Regina."

"What did she want?"

"To be my sister." That was the best answer he had.

"What does that mean?" Robert rolled over, keeping his eyes closed.

"It means I can always count on her to be the voice of reason." He hugged Robert to him.

Robert opened his eyes and Daniel met his gaze. "So what did she say?"

"First that I'm being a fool. You and I have talked about making Ashton Park our home, so that's what we're going to do. I promised that I'd help finance part of the renovations, and I used that money to fend off the attack on my company."

"You did what you had to do."

"I know. But my sister… look, I think I'm going to sell this condo, and I'll use the money to buy into the Ashton Park project." Daniel paused. "If I'm going to make Ashton Park my home in the future, then I need to do that. I can get a smaller place or a hotel when I come to New York. I don't need to keep this one, and with the money, we can probably get enough done to be able to open the house next spring. Part will be open to the public during certain times, and we'll live in other parts of the house."

"You don't have to do that." Robert leaned closer.

"Yes, I do. I need to put my money where my mouth is. If Ashton Park is going to be a home for both of us, then it needs to be something we're both committed to, and I am." He hugged him and Robert curled around him.

"How in the hell did I ever find you and what did I do to deserve you?"

Daniel was just thinking the same thing. "Come to think of it, we need to send Valerie an invitation to the wedding. After all, she should know how successful she was. I swear that woman must have ESP or something." It was hard to believe they'd hit a home run the first time at bat.

Robert pushed Daniel onto his back, rolling along with him until he pressed Daniel into the mattress. Robert's incredible eyes shone with delicious wickedness. "What am I going to do with you now that I have you right where I want you?"

"How about anything you want." Daniel leaned forward, attempting to capture Robert's lips, but he backed away before Daniel could reach them.

"I want you," Robert told him.

Daniel leaned forward again, and this time Robert didn't stop him. He pulled off his shirt and tugged open the buttons on Robert's, then tossed the shirts aside. He didn't watch as the fabric fluttered to the floor; he had something much more interesting to look at. "You can have me."

Robert rolled off the bed and stripped down to his boxers. Then he pulled open Daniel's pants, tugged them off, and added them to the growing pile of fabric on the bedroom floor. Robert prowled back up the bed, running his hands up Daniel's legs until they shook with anticipatory tension. He wanted Robert, and as soon as he was close enough, Daniel wrapped him in his arms, tugging Robert to him.

"This is so right." Daniel guided Robert's lips to his, tasting the man who had captured his heart.

Robert slipped his hands down Daniel's hips, pushing the fabric downward. Daniel kicked it off and bared himself to Robert, and not just because he was naked. He let go of his cares and let Robert see all of him. Daniel spent so much of his life in charge and making decisions that, as Robert took control, Daniel willingly gave it up, letting Robert be the master of their pleasure for a while.

"God…." Daniel groaned as Robert teased around his opening. He quivered a little as Robert increased the pressure, slipping a digit into his body. Instantly he wanted more, and Robert seemed to understand, stretching him. "I want you so bad."

Robert reached for the nightstand and found where Daniel kept lube and condoms. He straddled him, slicked his fingers, and slid them back inside. Daniel closed his eyes and let Robert's amazingly talented hands have their way with him.

"I hope this is okay."

"It's amazing." He tried to catch his breath, but Robert stole it again. And when Robert entered him, slowly filling him, Daniel saw double. This was erotic perfection. Robert stretched above him, his eyes shining, and when Robert kissed him, the energy that passed between them shocked him over and over. Daniel held on to Robert as though he were a lifeline, moving with him. "Don't you dare stop!"

Daniel grabbed Robert's butt cheeks, holding him tight, pushing him deep until his eyes crossed and he threw his head back, mouth wide open in a cry of ecstasy. His neighbors might have an issue, but at the moment, Daniel didn't give a damn. All that mattered was Robert.

"You feel bloody good, you know that?" Robert snapped his hips, sending Daniel into a spiral of bliss. Sex wasn't something he'd had a lot of in his life, and bottoming wasn't high on his list. But with Robert, the sensations that rolled through him were sublime—the stretch, the intensity in his eyes. Nothing else mattered in the least. Wherever Robert touched him, his skin came alive, and Daniel wanted more.

Robert held still, leaned forward, and kissed him hard. It was difficult not to keep moving, and soon the need overtook them both. Their kisses turned sloppy, but grew in intensity as Daniel's mind clouded and narrowed to only Robert.

"You're all I need." He gasped.

"How do you know?" Robert groaned hard and long.

"Because you're all I think about. All anyone has to do is mention your name and I want you, just like that." Daniel held on to Robert's shoulders, giving himself over to pure pleasure. Nothing else had ever compared to being with Robert, and the intensity of being together like this was more than he could take. When Robert added additional sensation, stroking him hard and fast, Daniel thought his head was going to explode. Together they barreled to completion like two runaway trains going out of control in the same direction. Only there was no crash at the end, just an airborne flight that sent Daniel sailing.

They stilled for a while and then settled on the bed. Robert left briefly to take care of business before joining him on the bed once again. "Sometimes you amaze me."

"What did I do so I can do it again?" Daniel propped his head on his hand, watching Robert. God, he'd never get tired of looking at this incredible man, the one he was in love with.

"You gave up your home for me... for us."

"No, I didn't. I gave up a New York apartment. That's all. I'm really coming to understand that home is where you are. For weeks I've thought of you, night and day. All someone had to do was ask about my trip and I was back with you at Ashton Park, walking the fields or sitting in the office. There was a storm a few days ago after I'd gone to bed and I turned to comfort you." That alone had told Daniel just how much Robert had come to mean to him in such a short time. "After it was over, I was glad you weren't here because it was a bad one, but I also missed just holding you."

Robert moved into his arms, and Daniel slipped his hand over Robert's belly, splaying his fingers to get as much touch as possible. "So I'll give up this apartment if it means I have the chance to build a home with you, wherever you want to make one."

Robert didn't give whatever his answer was, but in his heart, Daniel knew, especially from the conversation they'd had in England, that Robert wanted to live at Ashton Park.

"I have some things to finish up here in New York, but by the end of the week, I'll be ready to go back with you, if that works."

"Are you sure? After that fight, don't you need to stay here and see to things?"

"I will for a few days, and I'm going to have my technical guys develop some specifications so I can put together some additional meeting and teleconferencing capabilities. That means I can handle meetings remotely. The fight we just finished was over money and making a fast buck, not about the business and what we really do. Besides, those voices will be silenced." He was not going to put up with people who weren't in his corner. Daniel didn't want yes-men, but he didn't want people with their own agendas either.

"Are you sure that will be enough?"

"I may take one of the guys back with us to get everything set up at your house for now, if that's okay. We can move the equipment and connections to Ashton Park when we're ready."

Robert's eyes went a little googley. "You're serious."

"I am, and I want to set up a European division. It's a market that we can really expand into. A decade ago when Internet businesses were starting up in the US, Europe wasn't quite ready, but they are now, and being able to ship within the European Union is going to be an incredible advantage."

"I know better than to stand in your way. You have that look."

"What look?"

"The same one you had when you first said you'd marry me and that you'd help me with Ashton Park. I really think you can do anything."

"I wish. My reunion is in a few weeks and I'm still dreading the whole dang thing. In fact, I'm thinking that I don't want to go after all. Why bother? I used to want to impress those people, but I don't need to. I made something of myself, and it isn't likely they did more than take over their daddy's law practice or whatever they think is such hot shit."

"Of course you're going, and I'm going with you." Robert began to giggle. "Maybe I can find some medals or a few royal orders locked away someplace. There are some hereditary ones that I'm sure I belong to. I could put those on and walk into your reunion on your arm, and everyone will crap their pants."

"Fine. No royal orders, but I will take the part where you arrive on my arm." Daniel shifted slightly to get more comfortable and let the conversation drift off. Robert probably needed rest, and Daniel's mind wasn't going to stop running any time soon. Still, he had no intention of going anywhere for quite a while. He listened as Robert's breathing evened out and his body relaxed into sleep. Eventually Daniel, too, dozed off for a nap.

CHAPTER 9

THE LAST few weeks had been a whirlwind. Daniel had boundless energy for getting things contracted and started at Ashton Park. When they left, there had been plumbers, electricians, and even a company that specialized in the repair and installation of historically appropriate roofing.

Robert hung up the phone after speaking with Gene and turned to Daniel, who was just buttoning his shirt. Apparently Daniel's reunion was going to start with a luncheon gathering and then the more formal reception this evening. "Gene told me that we caught a bit of luck. The electrician told him that only one section of the house needs to be rewired. Apparently my uncle did have some updating done other than his apartment. The main areas of the house are fine. The below-stairs and third-floor areas need work, and they're being done. However, the plumbing is as bad as we feared."

"At least we caught a break somewhere. We can put the extra money into starting the worst areas of the roof."

"Already done," Robert said. "You're not the only one who can be a hurricane when necessary." He smiled as he brushed a few specks of lint off Daniel's shimmering silk shirt. "I love the way this feels."

"Me too. Regina designed these a few years ago, and yes, I know they aren't the latest fashion, but I adore them, so I got a few extras. I put one in your closet for you."

"We can't go in matching outfits." For a man who made his living in clothing and fashion retailing, sometimes Robert wondered about him.

"Of course not. But I wanted you to have one." Daniel swept Robert into his arms. "You'll look so wonderful in it, and I'll get the pleasure of stripping it off you." Daniel kissed him and then hugged him hard.

Robert knew Daniel was nervous—the energy rolled off him in waves. "You're a successful man, and you have no reason to be nervous or to feel anything other than proud of yourself." Robert held him in return. He knew the kind of memories these things could bring back. "Just have a good time."

"I'll do my best." Daniel stepped back and took a final look in the mirror. "I think I'm as ready as I'll ever be."

"I called the car service, and they'll be downstairs in five minutes." With Daniel's nervousness, Robert had figured he was going to be the organizer today. Daniel usually performed that role for them, seemingly without thinking. But Daniel had been scattered all day, so Robert had stepped in.

"Thanks." Daniel sighed. "I know I should have found a way to be out of the country."

"Come on. You're being overly dramatic, and that isn't like you. It's a lunch and then dinner, and then dancing this evening. You can make it through a single day, and then we'll fly back to Ashton Park tomorrow."

"I know." Daniel opened the door, and they left, moving toward the elevators.

The car was waiting when they got downstairs, and Robert hustled Daniel inside and told the driver to take them to the Plaza Hotel.

When they arrived, they were directed to a private ballroom. Daniel seemed even move nervous, so Robert took his arm. "It's going to be fine."

They stepped inside and Daniel stopped briefly. "They're all so old," he whispered.

"Of course they are. Did you think they stayed the same?" Robert wanted to laugh, but he remembered the last one of these that he'd gone to. He'd had the same reaction. In his mind, the guys from school had remained as he remembered them—that was, until he saw them again.

"Danny Boy?" a man asked as he hurried over. "It's Steven. I'm so glad you could make it." He clapped Daniel on the back and turned. "My wife, Constance."

Daniel's eyes widened as Constance, a statuesque woman of Latin descent, stepped forward. "It's a pleasure to meet you." Daniel turned to introduce him. "This is my fiancé, Robert Morton." They shook hands all around.

"What do you do, Daniel?" Constance asked in a lilted voice with a slight accent that added to her grace.

"Daniel started and runs Internet companies." Out of a new habit, Robert glanced down at the shoes Constance was wearing. "Western Couture and Kick in the Pants."

"Oh my goodness," one of the other women said. She must have overheard because she rushed over. "You made my favorite pair of boots." She showed off her footwear. "I love these to death."

"Thank you." Daniel looked lost for a second.

"Mattie Gordon. I'm Thomas's wife. He's over there at the bar." She seemed nice enough.

"Daniel Fabian, and this is my fiancé, Robert Morton. Do you know Steven and Constance Rhys-Jones? Steven is a lawyer, if I remember correctly."

"Yes. He manages the family law firm," Constance said as she took Steven's arm. Clearly it seemed it was the spouse's job to do the bragging at this gathering. "What do you do?"

"Robert is a barrister in a rural community in the English Midlands. Usually barristers are lawyers who argue cases in court, and solicitors handle legal documentation and processes, but Robert handles it all and is amazing to his community." Daniel turned to him, and Robert saw nothing but adoration. It didn't escape Robert's notice that Daniel didn't mention his title or the estate. "I think his accomplishments are pretty amazing."

"Oh my goodness." Mattie tittered. "That's really something."

"I love my work. I have an office that works with the people who need legal help the most. Lately I've had some success with larger clients, but it's fighting for regular people who are being taken advantage of by the system that I really sink my teeth into."

"So you don't have a large firm?" Constance asked, her nose turning upward slightly.

Robert knew that snobbish look very well. "No. I like helping people and taking the cases I want. That's something I could never do in a large firm. It's why my partners and I started the office in the first place."

"That sounds so... noble." She said the word as though it were something not to be mentioned in polite society.

"I'm very proud of him." Daniel put his hand around Robert's waist.

They continued chatting for a minute more, and then Constance found someone else she needed to speak to and guided Steven off in that direction.

"Don't mind her. She's all about who she thinks she can get to help Steven's career." Mattie rolled her eyes. "She's an infamous social climber." Mattie motioned, and Thomas joined them, handing her a drink.

"Tommy?" Daniel said with the first genuine smile Robert had seen since they left the apartment. "Man, it's good to see you."

"You too. I hear you're an Internet sensation."

"And Robert here is a barrister," Mattie chimed in. He and Thomas shook hands.

"Thomas is a photojournalist of sorts. I've read a number of your articles. I especially liked the one following a family of elephants for a year. It was amazingly gripping," Daniel said.

"We all have to do what we can." Thomas sipped his drink and looked over the ballroom. He was exceedingly tall and ruggedly handsome, where Mattie was a slight ball of energy. "I think they're motioning us to sit down."

They found a table together and were joined by others. Introductions were made, and thankfully Daniel didn't mention him being an earl. It didn't matter to him, and Mattie made sure everyone was well aware that he and Daniel were affianced. Through lunch, Daniel relaxed and talked to people around him. Robert learned a great deal about who Daniel had gone to school with, including who had been married four times already and who was having an affair with whom.

"New York society is an incestuous bunch," Mattie leaned over and whispered to him. "Everyone knows or knows of everyone, and they're all trying to get a leg up. It's like a pack of wolves." She turned to Thomas with near complete adoration.

"So how do you fit in?" Robert understood the ins and outs of society. His mother had made sure he was well educated in that way, even if they never actually mingled in it.

"I don't and I never truly will. They put up with me because Thomas's family is old New York money. But I'm just the poor girl he married because we fell in love." It was clear from the way Thomas gazed at his wife that he adored her. "So I ignore the bitches, have a good time, and stir things up whenever possible. It isn't like we're around all that often. Thomas and I are heading off to Australia for six months while he works on his next project." She caught the attention of a server and asked for a glass of water.

"If you're in England, you must look us up," Robert said and turned to Daniel, who was talking intently with Thomas. After all the nerves and apprehension Daniel had had about this event, it was so wonderful to see him relaxed having a good time.

Once lunch was over, Steven got up, welcomed everyone, and introduced his wife to everyone. Apparently she was the one who had actually organized everything, and she reviewed the evening's festivities. Trips to the Guggenheim had been arranged that afternoon for anyone who wished to go. That seemed to be mostly for the ladies, and apparently the men were gathering to play football of some sort in the park.

"Are you joining?" Thomas asked Daniel.

"No. I don't really need to relive my youth that way. You?"

He shook his head. "Then let's get a drink," Thomas offered, and they adjourned to the bar, where they found a table for four. "The last thing I need is to live through high school all over again." Thomas turned to Daniel. "I'm sorry I wasn't a better friend to you back then. We were all so wrapped up in things that seemed so important, when they really didn't mean a thing."

"What's past is past."

"Truthfully, I always admired you." The server interrupted them and took their drink orders. Thomas turned his attention back to Daniel as soon as he left. "You were always so independent and determined. No matter what the others did, you brushed it off and did your best to outshine them."

"Thomas, you're embarrassing him." Mattie took his arm.

"I'm only saying that you knew then what a lot of us are only starting to figure out. That it's better to go your own way that to follow the crowd off a cliff." The server brought their drinks, and Thomas raised his glass in a toast. "To the future."

"Amen to that," Daniel said, turning to him with a bright smile.

"So how did you meet?" Mattie asked.

Daniel set his drink on the table. "It was through a matchmaker...." He told them the story, with both Mattie and Thomas hanging on every word. Once again Robert noticed that there was no mention of his title or the estate.

"It sounds like a real, honest-to-goodness romance. I met Thomas when he was looking for an assistant." Her expression got very serious. "When I first met him, I thought he was a stuck-up little rich boy who always got whatever he wanted. He was fussy and a pain in the rear, but that was because he spent so much time in dangerous situations and it carried with him."

Robert turned to Thomas, whose adoring look for his wife never wavered for a second.

"He was stuck-up all right, but he found out he wasn't going to get everything he wanted from me." She leaned over the table, stage-whispering. "At least not until he showed me he had some manners. Then things fell into place."

"Yeah. All I had to do was admit that she was the one in charge." They all laughed, and Mattie leaned on his arm. "Have you decided where you're going to live?" Thomas asked.

"Robert recently inherited some family property, and he and I have decided that we're going to live there, once my visa goes through. I'm selling the place here in New York, and I'll probably get a small place or even stay in hotels when I'm in town. He needs to be in England for his work, and with technology I can work from just about anywhere, with regular visits to the office. I think it's going to be an amazing adventure."

Robert finished his drink and set his glass on the table. He sat back listening as Daniel and Thomas talked about some of the things they'd done in school. Mattie joined in occasionally, but mostly the two of them either chatted quietly or just listened to their reminiscences.

"We should get back to our hotel so we have time to get ready for dinner," Mattie reminded Thomas, and they all stood, saying good-bye until that night.

Daniel called the car service and asked the driver to take them home.

"Why didn't you tell them who I am? I thought that was part of the purpose of having me come with you to the reunion. It was what you said you wanted when we first met."

"I know, but things have changed. I don't need to be like them, and I certainly don't need their approval. I am proud of you for the man you are, and that's what's important." Daniel turned to watch out the window, and Robert waited for him to continue. "I think I realized something as I walked into that banquet hall. If what I loved about you was your title or the estate you live on, then I'd be no better than them. And I *am* better than they are. I've made something of myself. No one handed me a million dollars or anything else. I worked and earned what I have. And you did too. Yes, you inherited the estate, but before that, you built your law practice and you help people who need it every day."

"You're such an American, and I mean that in the best way possible. You value hard work and determination over class and the place you're born into."

"I guess I forgot that for a while."

"I don't think so. You just got caught up in what so many people do. It's easy to try to show people up, but it only makes you seem like the better person for a few minutes. Then reality kicks in and you realize you diminished yourself without even knowing it." Robert shifted closer to Daniel on the seat. "If you don't want to tell them, then I won't. It doesn't matter to me."

"Me neither. All that matters is you." Daniel held him close, and they rode in the stop-and-go, near-gridlock traffic to the apartment. Still, because he was with Daniel, it was the shortest ride in history. And when Daniel leaned close to his ear….

"I love you, Robert Morton."

"And I love you."

"Could you drive us through the park?" Daniel asked, and the driver made the turns.

"What about the rest of the reunion?" Robert settled on the seat.

"I have all I want right here." Daniel raised the privacy screen and kissed him hard.

EPILOGUE

The following May

THE WEATHER was extraordinary, and Daniel was about ready to explode with excitement.

"When did you wake up this morning?" Regina asked over her morning cup of coffee in the private kitchen of Ashton Park.

"He was awake sometime around four," Robert said as he half stumbled in to join them. "Now I understand why he looks the way he does." Robert kissed him and ruffled Daniel's hair. "But I have to say that no one should ever look as put together as you do at seven in the morning."

"Oh, this," she said, looking down at herself, and Daniel snorted.

"Regina never goes anywhere or is seen by anyone without being dressed to the nines. I swear she came down the birth canal in a little tiny black-and-white Chanel suit and has been making herself up ever since." Daniel grabbed his mug of coffee and got out of the way of her light-handed swipe.

"What time is the opening?"

"Ten o'clock, and we've promoted the heck out of it in all the local papers, as well as on a number of tourist sites, so we're hoping we'll get a good crowd." Daniel had agonized over how much to charge to tour Ashton Park, and they had settled on twelve pounds. He didn't want it to be too expensive, but he also didn't want them to price the tour too cheaply. It was guided, and they had done their best to make sure it would be an experience.

"Then we better get dressed and do one final walk-through." Robert put his mug in the sink and went to their bedroom, and Daniel followed and closed the door behind them. "How should I look?"

174

"Like the lord of the manor. Today you're playing the part of the Earl of Hantford, so dress accordingly. Maybe something in tweed."

"Please. I'll look nice, and you can have a name tag made for me that says 'Robert, Earl of Hantford.'" He rolled his eyes, and Daniel groaned. They changed clothes and then left their room to tour the more gracious and grand portions of the house.

The hall looked splendid with its paintings, its rich wood, and the gleaming chandelier hung overhead. For some reason it had never been electrified and they had elected to leave it that way. The candles were fresh, and while they wouldn't be lit, the crystals glimmered with the light through the windows.

"I love how this turned out." Robert looked around.

"I do too, and we can have the ancestral paintings cleaned and restored as we go." They had wanted to do some of the conservation work on the artwork in the estate, but there wasn't enough money for all of it at the moment.

Daniel opened the door to the library and marveled as he always did at how incredible it turned out. The deep red curtains hung almost sixteen feet high. The rug on the floor was a reproduction of the original. They'd had it milled for the house so that during tours, the reproduction could be used, but when the house wasn't open for tours, he and Robert could enjoy the original. The bookcases were full, the books from storage back in their rightful places, and each one had been catalogued, with many priceless volumes in the collection, including a few manuscripts and an early edition of Shakespeare.

But what always drew Daniel's eye every time he entered the library was the impressive bronze stag on the center table and then the Turner landscape that hung high over the fireplace. Again, during tours, a very authentic reproduction hung, and the original was safely stored in a temperature- and humidity-controlled vault that Daniel had had built on the property.

"This always takes my breath away."

They continued through to the morning room, the dining room, and the various sitting and living rooms, which had all been cleaned and restored as best they could at the moment. There were still items on their list to accomplish, but each room was impressive.

They ended their tour in the study, and once again Daniel was so happy, he rolled back on his heels. The paneling had been carefully cleaned, and the artwork hung properly. This was probably his favorite room in the house—and the one, besides their bedroom, where he and Robert had made love the most.

"Get those thoughts out of your head." Robert raised his gaze. "We don't have time. The docents will be arriving at any minute for last instructions, and I definitely don't want your sister catching us with our trousers down."

"I was only thinking."

"I know woodwork makes you hot."

Robert's teasing wasn't so far off. This room was masculine in its entirety, and maybe that was why he was always dragging Robert there. Either that or he was just one horny bastard.

"What can I do to help?" Regina asked as she came through the door off the hall, and Robert flashed him an "I told you so" look.

"Check that the bedrooms upstairs that are being shown are ready and perfect. They'll go up the back stairs and exit down the main stairs and then out of the house. Be fussy and let us know if anything is out of place."

"Will do." She went upstairs, and they returned to the hall.

"So what is my job for today?" Robert asked.

"You will be stationed in the library and can welcome visitors. We aren't going to do that normally, but since it's opening day, we want people to be talking about us. So seeing you might help. I'll be overseeing everything and making adjustments if needed." Daniel checked the time as some of their staff began arriving. They had trained eight docents to give tours, with four or five going at any one time.

"I'm ready to go," Isabelle said as she entered the hall like a breath of fresh air. She had agreed to be the head docent and manage the flow of tours and people. "There are already dozens of vehicles in the car park, and even a bus has pulled in." She patted each of them on the cheek. "This old place looks better than I remember. You have both done a remarkable job, and I'm so proud of both my boys."

"The bedrooms are perfect," Regina said as she came down the stairs. "I'm going out to check on ticket sales and make sure everything is ready at the gate." She was off like the dervish she was, and Isabelle hurried to where she had told her staff to meet her. Gene and his brothers came in to say they were ready and on standby in case anything came up, and then hurried out again.

"I never thought this would actually happen," Robert said when the hall was empty for a few minutes. "And it wouldn't have if it weren't for you." He reached into his pocket and pulled out one of the brass name badges that Daniel had had made up for all the staff and pinned it on Robert's chest.

"What did you do?" Daniel lifted the tag that read "Count of Hantford." He and Robert rarely used their titles with anyone. It wasn't the way they wanted to live their lives. "Are you sure?"

"Yes. It's a courtesy title, but the proper one and you've earned it. Besides, I want everyone to know that you're taken in case anyone gets any ideas." Robert double-fisted his husband's shirt, tugged him close, and kissed him. "I love you more than I ever thought possible, Count of Hantford."

"And I you, Robert, Earl of Hantford. But as far as I'm concerned, you're the prince of my heart." Daniel returned Robert's kiss as one of the doors behind them opened and closed.

"Please, will you two stop with the kissy face? There are so many people lined up that we're going to get tours started. I have docents that are going to be out front in five minutes."

Isabelle hurried away and Robert stepped back. "It looks like I'm off to the library."

"And I'm going to check out front. But later I'll give you your own private tour." Daniel stepped very close to Robert. "And it will definitely end in the study." He winked and heard Robert's breath hitch.

"I'll look forward to it."

Daniel would too, and many more amazing days to come with the earl who had stolen his heart.

ANDREW GREY grew up in western Michigan with a father who loved to tell stories and a mother who loved to read them. Since then he has lived all over the country and traveled throughout the world. He has a master's degree from the University of Wisconsin-Milwaukee and now works full-time on his writing. Andrew's hobbies include collecting antiques, gardening, and leaving his dirty dishes anywhere but in the sink (particularly when writing). He considers himself blessed with an accepting family, fantastic friends, and the world's most supportive and loving husband. Andrew currently lives in beautiful historic Carlisle, Pennsylvania.

E-mail: andrewgrey@comcast.net
Website: www.andrewgreybooks.com

CAN'T LIVE
WITHOUT YOU

ANDREW
GREY

Justin Hawthorne worked hard to realize his silver-screen dreams, making his way from small-town Pennsylvania to Hollywood and success. But it hasn't come without sacrifice. When Justin's father kicked him out for being gay, George Miller's family offered to take him in, but circumstances prevented it. Now Justin is back in town and has come face to face with George, the man he left without so much as a good-bye… and the man he's never stopped loving.

Justin's disappearance hit George hard, but he's made a life for himself as a home nurse and finds fulfillment in helping others. When he sees Justin again, George realizes the hole in his heart never mended, and he isn't the only one in need of healing. Justin needs time out of the public eye to find himself again, and George and his mother cannot turn him away. As they stay together in George's home, old feelings are rekindled. Is a second chance possible when everything George cares about is in Pennsylvania and Justin must return to his career in California? First they'll have to deal with the reason for Justin's abrupt departure all those years ago.

www.dreamspinnerpress.com

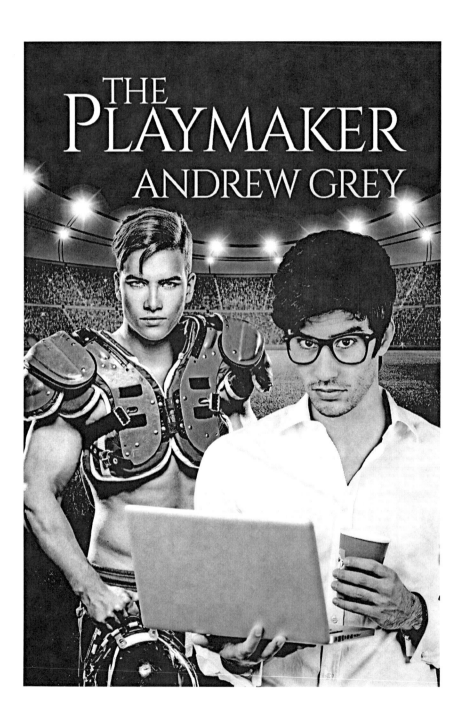

THE
PLAYMAKER
ANDREW GREY

Professional football player Hunter Davis is learning that saying he's gay is very different from actively being in a relationship with another man—especially in the eyes of his teammates and fans. So when Hunter needs a personal assistant to keep him organized, he asks for a woman in order to prevent tongues from wagging.

Montgomery Willis badly needs to find work before he loses everything. There's just one position at the agency where he applies, but the problem is, he's not a woman. And he knows nothing about football. Still, Hunter gives him a chance, but only because Monty's desperate.

Monty soon proves his worth by saving Hunter's bacon on an important promotional shoot, and Hunter realizes he might have someone special working for him—in more ways than one. Monty's feelings come to the surface during an outing in the park when Hunter decides to teach Monty a bit about the game, and pictures surface of them in some questionable positions. Hunter is reminded that knowing he's gay and seeing evidence in the papers are two very different things for the other players, and he might have to choose between two loves: football and Monty.

www.dreamspinnerpress.com

ANDREW GREY

TURNING
the PAGE

Malcolm Webber is still grieving the loss of his partner of twenty years to cancer. He's buried his mind and feelings in his legal work and isn't looking for another relationship. He isn't expecting to feel such a strong attraction when he meets Hans Erickson—especially since the man is quite a bit younger than him.

Hans is an adventure writer with an exciting lifestyle to match. When he needs a tax attorney to straighten out an error with the IRS, he ends up on the other side of the handsome Malcolm's desk. The heat between them is undeniable, but business has to come first. When it's concluded, Hans leaps on the chance to make his move.

Malcolm isn't sure he's ready for the next chapter in his life. Hans is so young and active that Malcolm worries he won't be able to hold his interest for long. Just when he's convinced himself to take the risk and turn the page, problems at the law office threaten to end their love story before it can really begin.

www.dreamspinnerpress.com

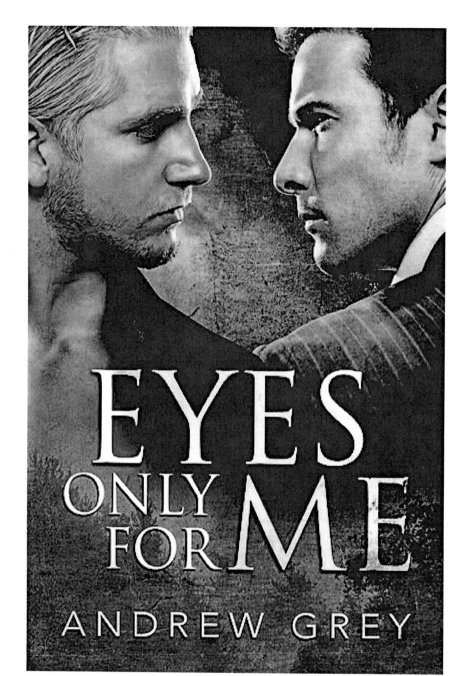

EYES
ONLY
FOR ME

ANDREW GREY

Eyes of Love: Book One

For years, Clayton Potter's been friends and workout partners with Ronnie. Though Clay is attracted, he's never come on to Ronnie because, let's face it, Ronnie only dates women.

When Clay's father suffers a heart attack, Ronnie, having recently lost his dad, springs into action, driving Clay to the hospital over a hundred miles away. To stay close to Clay's father, the men share a hotel room near the hospital, but after an emotional day, one thing leads to another, and straight-as-an-arrow Ronnie make a proposal that knocks Clay's socks off! Just a little something to take the edge off.

Clay responds in a way he's never considered. After an amazing night together, Clay expects Ronnie to ignore what happened between them and go back to his old life. Ronnie surprises him and seems interested in additional exploration. Though they're friends, Clay suddenly finds it hard to accept the new Ronnie and suspects that Ronnie will return to his old ways. Maybe they both have a thing or two to learn.

www.dreamspinnerpress.com

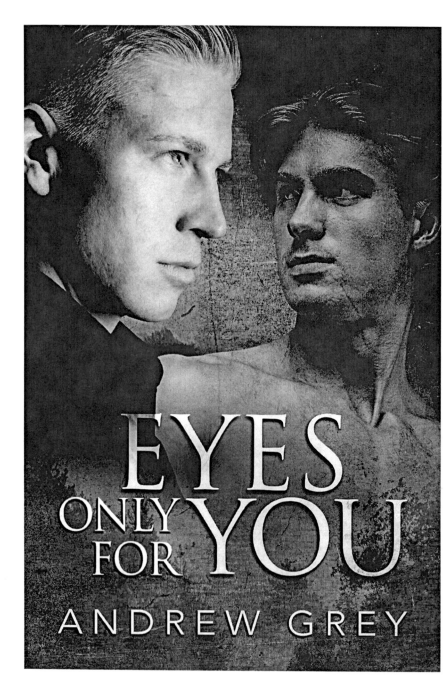

EYES
ONLY YOU
FOR

ANDREW GREY

Sequel to *Eyes Only for Me*
Eyes of Love: Book Two

Marcello Bagnini has a history of falling for the wrong men, and it seems he's done it again. Working out at the gym with his straight friend Jerry is becoming harder by the day—in more ways than one. Worse yet, Jerry isn't the only one who notices Marcello's wandering eyes. So instead of risking his friendship with Jerry and alienating the other guys at the gym, Marcello keeps his feelings to himself.

Real estate agent Jerry Foland has never explored his interest in other men, but there's something different about Marcello, and Jerry's starting to think he might like to see where his attraction could lead. However, Jerry's controlling father makes it clear that it's either stay on the straight and narrow or Jerry can say good-bye to his family.

As much as they try to stay away from each other, their lives overlap, both at the gym and when Jerry is contracted to sell the home of one of Marcello's friends. Friendship grows into more, but Jerry's father has his own agenda, and it doesn't include having a gay son.

www.dreamspinnerpress.com

CPSIA information can be obtained
at www.ICGtesting.com
Printed in the USA
FSOW02n0739090117
29408FS